THE DOUBLE CROSS

A TRAVELERS PREQUEL NOVELLA

MICHAEL P. KING

BLURRED LINES PRESS

Blurred Lines Press

The Double Cross

Michael P. King

ISBN 978-0-9861796-9-3

Cover design by Paramita Bhattacharjee at creativeparamita.com

A con artist betrayed by his partners. A plot for revenge. Can he and his new partner outwit his old crew... and escape with the cash and their lives?

In 1989, where it all begins...

Paul Kendal, 26 years old, is a con artist in a robbery crew. When he has all the information necessary to disarm their targets' alarm systems and empty their safes, his partners go to work.

Originally, it seemed like a sweet plan, but as he begins to have doubts, his partners double-cross him. Now he wants payback. For that he needs a new partner.

Carol, 17 years old, uses her movie-star good looks to entice victims for her boyfriend to mug. But when her boyfriend lands in jail, Paul makes her an offer she can't refuse...

The Double Cross is a novella-length, hard-hitting crime thriller that tells the story of how the Travelers met. If you like fast moving action, unpredictable plot twists, and criminal chicanery, you'll love this prequel to Michael P. King's Travelers series.

For Sarah

1

MAY 1989

Paul Kendal was worried about his partners. He'd fallen in with this robbery crew about a year ago, hoping to sharpen his skills, but now he was beginning to wonder if it was worth it. The crew—Jacob, Stevie, and Pooch—were all older guys who had met up in prison. Jacob, their leader, almost fifty, had the ropey arms and sunken chest of a long-term alcoholic. He was the safe cracker. Stevie, red-gray hair and freckles, a burn scar on his arm from the car wreck that landed him in prison the first time, was the driver. And Pooch, a bald army veteran who'd gone to fat, was the weapons guy. They were tired of being busted back to prison—too old to do the time anymore—so instead of breaking and entering commercial buildings with their ever more complicated alarm systems, they were on the prowl for wealthy older women with valuables in home safes.

That's why they'd recruited Paul. He was twenty-six years old, dark-haired, and ruggedly handsome. He seduced the lonely widows or divorcees who were willing to believe, hope against hope, that they had finally found love. And when he had all the information necessary to successfully complete the job, his partners went to work. Originally, it had seemed like a sweet plan. But as time went on, and they bounced from town to town, Paul thought they were taking too many risks—risks that fell disproportionately on him.

And here they were again, gathered under a streetlight in a gravel parking lot, this time at the Vine Club in Madisonville, making their last preparations for their current score.

"It's too soon," Paul said.

"Look," Jacob said, "we've got the safe specs. We know where the rest of the goodies are. It's time to do this job."

"I've got a bad feeling about this," Paul replied. "I need a couple more weeks to set the bona fides."

Stevie snorted. "Listen to you. You're sleeping in her bed. Wearing that new watch she bought you. Driving her car. How much more trust do you need?"

"Guys, I'm the new boyfriend. I'm the one who's going to be arrested if it all goes south. I need more time."

"Paul," Jacob said, "we brought you in to our crew because you got a gift for bamboozling old broads. That doesn't make you a decision-maker. Are you going to do your part?"

Paul frowned. "I'll do my part. I told you guys I'd do it, and I will."

"Okay, then. Quit your bitching. We're doing this job tomorrow. Make sure she's out of the house and the alarm is turned off."

Pooch slapped him on the shoulder. "Don't worry, kid. Just hold her hand and wipe her tears. You'll be fine."

"And don't forget, we changed the rendezvous. We're meeting at the Travel Ace motel in Liberty Ridge," Jacob said. "If it takes you more than a week to slip away, we'll leave a note at the desk. You've got nothing to worry about. This is all cake."

"Okay," Paul said. "I'll see you guys in Liberty Ridge."

Paul crossed the parking lot to a red Oldsmobile. These guys never listened. They were going to keep pushing until one of these jobs blew up. Why should they care? They weren't the ones who'd be going to prison. After this score—after he had his cut—maybe it was time for him to go his own way. He took a right out of the parking lot just after a beat-up Chevy Malibu went by. He was tired of this con anyway. Some of the women deserved what they got. They were selfish and self-centered, always ready to take advantage. But some of the others were just lonely and gullible. Like their current mark. Cicilie Chandler was such a sweet woman. It was surprising she didn't have a man. When she came home and found her house burglarized, she'd be terrified at the thought that someone had been rifling through her drawers. He pulled into the left-turn lane at the intersection with Orchid Street. But he couldn't back out now. The guys were counting on him, and he'd given his word. She was wealthy. She had insurance on her valuables. And he'd make it up to her. Before he left, he'd help her pick a better home security system and better locks—make sure she felt safe in her home. That would be his gift to her.

JACOB, Stevie, and Pooch watched Paul drive away. "Hey," Pooch said, "I thought we were going to Emmett City."

"We are," Jacob said. "I'm done listening to him complain. We're going to split his end and move on."

"If we're going to keep his end," Stevie said, "we need to make sure he won't be coming after us."

"I'll make an anonymous phone call to Chandler's partner," Jacob said. "He's got a reputation for having a bad temper."

Pooch stuck his hands in his pockets. "I don't know, guys. Maybe we should cut the kid some slack—give him his share and turn him loose."

"Are you kidding?" Stevie asked.

"Fuck him," Jacob said. "He's not one of us. It was always going to come to this. He's the only face connected to the jobs we've pulled. And I don't need the whining aggravation. We'll find a new guy to sweet-talk the ladies."

THE NEXT MORNING, Cicilie Chandler woke up lying next to Paul in her king-size, canopied bed. Cicilie's late husband, Dan, had started out in banking, but before his heart attack, he'd branched out into construction and real estate, so he could finance, build, and sell. He'd done very well, and he had left Cicilie a silent partnership in a lucrative business. She'd been a bathing suit beauty in her youth. Now she was soft and round, in good shape for a fifty-two-year-old woman, but still embarrassed when Paul saw her without any clothes. She pulled the silk sheet around her breasts before she snuggled against his side. He opened his eyes and slipped his arm around her shoulders.

"Good morning, beautiful."

She blushed. He said it every day, but she still wasn't used to it. "Every morning when I wake up, I expect you to be gone."

"Still here." He kissed her. "What's on your agenda today?"

"Into the office to sign some papers so that Sam can get started on the condos out by the airport. Then off to the spa. Bridge this afternoon with the girls. What about you? You have time for lunch?"

"Sorry. I've got golf with Kevin Chou. I think he's just about ready to buy that new house."

"Out on Putnam Lake? I've known his wife for years. Do you want me to put in a word?"

"Cissy, we've talked about this."

"I just want to help."

"I know you do, but I'm a guy, remember. You already do too much for me." He gave her a squeeze.

"What do you want to do about dinner?" she asked.

"I could cook."

"Nonsense. What about the new steakhouse on Royal Road?"

"Hickory Forge?"

"Uh-huh. Margie was there last week. She loved it."

"Okay, let's give it a try."

THAT EVENING PAUL and Cicilie were seated at a window table in the Hickory Forge steakhouse on the west edge of town just past Putnam Lake. The interior was dark wood, white tablecloths, candles, and low lights. They were sitting catty-corner and holding hands under the table. Cicilie liked to bring Paul to places like this, where she could feel romantic without worrying that everyone was staring at them. If their ages were reversed, no one would think anything of a man her age being involved with a woman his age. Paul lifted her hand, kissed it, and let go.

He peered down the menu. "What are you going to have?"

"I know it's crazy to eat fish in a steakhouse, but I'm having the salmon."

"I thought about it, but I'm going for the rib eye."

"How did your golf go?"

"Great. I crushed Kevin. Might have hurt my chances on the sale, but I can't let anyone win. They have to beat me. What about you? Spa good?"

"The new massage therapist is really excellent. You should try him sometime."

"Massage is not my thing."

She laughed. "You mean massage from a man is not your thing."

"Touché. What about the bridge game?"

"We barely started. You remember Betty Roberts?"

"Blonde woman with the old-fashioned hairdo?"

She nodded. "Her husband's divorcing her. Their youngest is off to college at the end of the summer. She had no idea. The coward packed up his clothes while she was out and then told her over the phone."

"She really had no idea?"

"Well, I don't know how much time they spent together. He was always at work—or that's what he said."

"Did he admit to having a girlfriend?"

"She said that he said the spark just wasn't there anymore. Then she started crying. It was horrible."

"If there's no girlfriend, and she wants him back, she needs a makeover."

"She does dress a little matronly, but—"

Their server, a young woman wearing a uniform of white shirt with black pants, stepped up to the table with their martinis and then took their orders. After she left, Cicilie continued. "The clothes, the hair—do you really think it makes that much difference? They were married, had children—"

"Maybe he's looking for some excitement. Maybe he doesn't want to believe he's middle-aged. It's not a fair comparison. You've always been one of the pretty girls, but look at the difference between you and her. I imagine you're about the same age, but she almost looks old enough to be your mother."

"She doesn't look *that* old."

"Maybe you just look that young."

She pushed his shoulder. "Stop it."

"It's not flattery if it's true."

MEANWHILE, at Cicilie's house on Fillmore Drive, Jacob, Stevie, and Pooch had parked a stolen plumber's van at the top of the drive and gone in through the front door as if they were making an emergency service call. The house, a two-story white brick with a wraparound porch, was located in the old-money part of town. The houses were large, traditional structures, remodeled for all the modern conveniences, and set back from the street, guaranteeing the privacy everyone valued.

Pooch was in the master bedroom. He moved systematically through the space, starting with the closet, searching through the clothes and boxes on the shelves for any cash or small items that had been hidden away. Nothing. He moved on to the dresser, where he found a drawer of loose jewelry: three rings, five sets of earrings, and two watches—the day-to-day stuff. He scooped them into his pocket. All done here. As he turned, he glanced at the four-poster canopy bed, with its tied-back gauze curtains and lacey pillow covers. It was a fantasy out of a women's magazine. He thought about Paul banging the old lady doggy-style and chuckled.

Down in the basement, Jacob was working on the safe. It was an ancient, easy model, three numbers, so he was cracking it old-school by listening for the tumblers and making a graph to reveal the six possible combinations. He was almost there.

Bingo. He opened the door. There were the usual legal papers: a stack of savings bonds—too tough to fence—and an accordion envelope of banded one-hundred-dollar bills, maybe twenty thousand total, and five jewelry boxes. He opened the top box. It contained a beautiful emerald necklace. He slipped the envelope and the jewelry boxes into an empty plumber's toolbox and closed the safe door. Then he stepped over to the burglar alarm control box and tripped the alarm. *That would fix the kid.*

On the first floor, Stevie was watching the street and listening to a portable police scanner. Pooch came down the stairs and gave the thumbs-up sign. The phone rang. They searched through the first floor until they found the answering machine in the kitchen. Stevie played back the message. "ADT Security. Please pick up."

Pooch jogged over to the stairs to the basement. "Jacob, cops are on their way."

Jacob rushed up the stairs. They scurried out the kitchen door, jogged through the backyard past the bird feeders and a trellis of roses, and cut through the neighbor's yard. No one was on the street. A Dodge Charger was parked at the curb. They piled into the car, Stevie behind the wheel. A police car, lights on, siren off, sped past them while they sat at a stop sign. Pooch chuckled.

"Don't jinx it," Jacob said. "We still need to collect our gear and get out of town."

PAUL AND CICILIE were walking across the parking lot of the Hickory Forge steakhouse when a Silver SUV squealed to a stop in front of them. Sam Bryant, Cicilie's business partner—a tall, thin, black man dressed in golfing clothes—jumped out of the front seat passenger's side. "Cicilie."

"Sam. What's this about?"

"Your house has been robbed."

"What?" She clutched Paul's arm. Two men wearing black suits and the hard looks of hired guns got out of the SUV.

Sam continued. "The police are there now. Your alarm kicked over. The cops found a plumber's van in your driveway."

Paul gave the hired guns a quick glance. Something was wrong. His partners couldn't have accidentally tripped the alarm. He'd turned it off. Time to play the concerned boyfriend. "We should get back to your house."

Sam shook his head. "We need to talk first."

Paul tried for a quizzical expression. He had to play this very carefully. Cicilie wouldn't just dismiss the concerns of the man who'd been her husband's best friend. "What's this all about?"

"I've got some questions. I want answers."

Paul glanced at the hired guns. They were positioning themselves so that they could catch him if he tried to run. He doubted that they would let him leave with Cicilie. His best chance was to play along. "Okay, I get it. I'm the new guy. You feel protective. What do you want to know?"

"Get in the car."

"I'm coming with you," Cicilie said.

"I don't think that's a good idea," Sam said.

"I don't care."

They drove in silence north of town to a new subdivision where the sewer lines were being laid and pulled up to a large work trailer at the front of the property. "Why are we here?" Cicilie asked.

"Just needed some privacy," Sam said. "Quicker than driving to the office."

One of Sam's men unlocked the trailer. Inside was a kitchenette, a long folding table surrounded by metal folding chairs, a row of lockers, and a washroom. "Why don't you sit down, Cicilie?" Sam pulled out a folding chair for her.

The hired guns moved Paul around to a chair at the far end of the table. "This isn't necessary," Paul said. "I want to help."

"I'm sure you do," Sam said. "You've been dating Cicilie for about a month? Is that correct?"

"Yeah."

"What's this about, Sam?" Cicilie asked.

"I got a phone call—an anonymous tip—that Paul is mixed up in the robbery."

"Paul? That's just not possible."

Sam knelt in front of Cicilie and put his hand on her shoulder. "Unfortunately, it is possible. That's the world we live in. I'm sorry. It would be better if you waited in the car."

"No, I can't believe it."

"You're a quality person, Cicilie. You want to see the best in people. I hope I'm wrong. When I saw how happy you were, I really hoped. But I had Marty run a background check on this guy. He's not a good person."

"I don't know what you mean by that."

"I promised Dan that I would protect you no matter what. And that's what I'm going to do. Please go out to the car."

"No."

"Sam," Paul said, "this is crazy. If you think I had something to do with the robbery, turn me over to the police."

"They wouldn't arrest you. There's no evidence."

One of the hired guns said, "Empty your pockets."

"No," Paul said.

"You want to get smacked around before we start? Empty your pockets."

Paul emptied his pockets onto the table: wallet, car keys, and a pocketknife. The hired guns pushed him down onto a folding chair and tied his arms and legs to the chair with plastic ties. Then they tipped the chair back onto the floor. The nearest man looked up at Sam. He nodded. The other man wrung out a hand towel in the sink and picked up a five-gallon jug of water from the counter.

Cicilie's face was white. Her hands trembled. "These guys don't work for us."

"No," Sam said. "I hired them special."

"So you were expecting you would need them even before my house was robbed."

"Like I said, the background check looked pretty grim. But I wasn't going to do anything if there was any chance I was wrong."

Paul looked from the man kneeling beside him to the man standing with the water. "Hey, guys, don't you have some questions?"

"We're just going to get your attention first," the kneeling man said.

The man with the jug tossed the damp towel to the kneeling man, who stretched the towel over Paul's face. The man with the jug poured the water out onto the towel. Paul kicked and struggled. The chair banged against the floor. When the kneeling man removed the towel, Paul choked, gasped, and spat up water.

"Do we need to go again?"

Paul was red-faced. He shook his head. "No. I'll tell you—I'll tell you anything."

"Stop it," Cicilie yelled. "Stop it. This is insane."

"Shush," Sam said. "I know this is hard. If I'm wrong, I'll apologize. I'll make it right. Maybe he's just a gigolo. Maybe he's got nothing to do with the robbery. I'll write him a check. Pay his medical bills. But I'm going to know the truth before he leaves here."

"You just can't believe he really loves me."

"I wish it was so. I really do. I just don't believe in this much coincidence." He looked down at Paul. "I've got all night. I'm going to know the truth. Are you working with the robbers?"

Paul looked from Sam to the hired guns kneeling over him, and then to Cicilie. There was no point in lying. Their relationship was over. "Yes."

Cicilie began to sob. "I don't believe it. He'd say anything to make you stop."

"We weren't going to hurt her," Paul said. "I wouldn't let anyone hurt her. That's why I was with her—to make sure she was safe."

"Somehow, your words don't mean much now," Sam said. He turned to Cicilie. "I should take you home. You're the victim here. No one needs to know about this guy. It will just raise a lot of embarrassing questions."

She looked at Paul. "Oh, my God. How could you—I let you—" She started sobbing again.

"I'm sorry. I really am."

Sam turned to the hired guns. "Find out what you can." He helped Cicilie to her feet. "Let's go."

"What are you going to do with him?"

"You don't want to know."

"You can't kill him."

"He's just going to go off and do the same thing again."

"I don't care. Promise me."

Sam nodded. "I promise." He turned to the hired guns. "You heard her."

"You're the boss," the closest man said.

Sam led Cicilie out of the trailer. Paul watched her leave. No witnesses now. "I'll tell you whatever you want to know."

"Where are your partners?"

"I was supposed to catch up with them in a couple of weeks."

"That's no answer."

"They put an ad in the paper. That way if I get caught, I can't give them up, and if they get caught, they can't give me up."

"That story is too complicated."

The man on his right stood up and kicked him in the head; then the one on his left kicked him in the side. They took turns kicking him, yelling for him to tell the truth and kicking him, but he stuck to his story until he lost consciousness. When he woke up, he was lying in the bed of a pickup truck in the dark. The sky was full of stars, and the night was quiet except for the crickets. The men lowered the tailgate, dragged him out of the bed of the truck, and pitched him into a ditch. He rolled into the weeds. One of them said, "Stay away from Mrs. Chandler."

The hired guns drove away. Paul lay there a few minutes. He hurt all over. He wasn't sure if he could stand, but he didn't want to be there if they changed their minds and came back. Which way was back to town? The way those guys had gone? He crawled up the bank. Off in the distance, across a soybean field, he saw headlights. Another road. He pulled himself to his feet. He was bent over, his hands on his knees. He thought he was a pretty good liar. Had those guys believed him? He felt so sorry for Cicilie. She couldn't possibly understand that he actually had cared for her. That's the only way he could really sell it. He had to care and not care, both at the same time—the caring on the outside and the not caring on the inside. He started across the soybean field, limping and holding his ribs.

A few hours later, he came to an intersection at the edge of town. On one corner was a Phillips gas station. Across the road a flashing sign said "Mickey's Rodeo." The gas station parking lot was empty; the honky-tonk's parking lot was full. The gas station bathroom was on the side of the building. The light was bright, the floor was more or less clean, and the mirror over the sink wasn't broken. Paul looked at himself. There was a big bruise at his hairline and blood under his nose. He washed his face, combed his fingers through his hair, and wiped off his clothes with a damp paper towel. He looked like he'd been sleeping on a bench, but it would have to do.

He walked across the road to Mickey's Rodeo. The bouncer, a pumped-up guy with a look in his eye like he'd just been released from prison, gave him a hard glare but didn't stop him from entering. The place was crowded, and the lights were dim. Top-forty country music blasted from the jukebox. He needed to call Pooch to come get him, but his cash and wallet were back at that trailer or in one of those assholes' pockets. At the end of the bar, three couples stood together, trying to signal the bartender. He changed his gait to appear drunk, stumbled into one of the men, and lifted the wallet from the handbag of the woman next to him. "Sorry, sorry," he said, "my mistake."

He staggered to the pay phone and used the change from the woman's wallet. "Pooch, glad I caught you. You guys tripped the alarm. Cicilie's partner set some guys on me. They dumped me out north of town. Come and get me."

"You're supposed to be dead."

"Supposed to be?"

"You don't get it, kid. Jacob dimed you out."

"Why? Why would he do that?"

"You don't know anything, do you?"

"I want my share from the job."

"Look, I like you, kid, but if you come around here, you're going to get shot. You shouldn't have been mouthing off to Jacob, giving him a headache. Take it as a lesson and move on." He hung up.

Paul turned from the phone. His mouth tasted like ashes. He never should have trusted those guys. He was always the outsider with them. Now they'd double-crossed him, and there was nothing he could do about it. At least for now. He shifted his weight. Pain shot down his leg from his lower back. He needed to lie down before he fell down. He started out of the bar. At the door he turned to the bouncer. "Hey, buddy, I found this wallet on the floor back by the restrooms." He handed the bouncer the woman's wallet. Out in the parking lot, he walked around to the side of the building where he couldn't be seen, found an unlocked car, and hotwired it.

He left the car on the street one block over from his rent-by-the-week motel room. The parking lot was full. He scanned the cars. There was no one watching the room. How to get in? No deadbolt, just the cheapest lockset that could be bought in bulk. He glanced around on the sidewalk for a thin piece of metal or a stiff piece of plastic. No such luck. He didn't want to go down to the office and wake up the manager. Screw it. He gave the door the best kick he had. It swung open. There was no one sitting on the bed with a gun in hand. He looked back at the doorframe. The latch plate and a few inches of wood were pushed out of the frame. He closed the door. He looked under the mattress. His hammerless Smith & Wesson .38 snub-nose and an envelope containing $200 were still there. He put the pistol in his front pants pocket and the envelope in his back pocket. His head was swimming. He wasn't sure how he'd managed to drive here. He shuffled two steps and fell on the bed.

EARLY MORNING, Jacob, Stevie, and Pooch were at a Best Western motel at a freeway interchange outside Emmett City. They'd rented two rooms with a pass-through door. Three prostitutes posed on the beds in their underwear with drinks in their hands while Stevie used a razor blade to lay out lines of cocaine on the glass-topped table. He snorted a line, and then held up the straw. Pooch went next. Then he handed the straw to Jacob. "That's some good shit."

"I told you that guy wasn't an asshole," Stevie said.

"Well, you said you knew a guy who knew a guy, which didn't inspire a whole lot of confidence," Jacob said.

Pooch wiped at his nose. "The kid reached out to me."

"And you said?"

"He better not show."

Stevie looked up from laying out some more lines. "Think he's going to make trouble?"

"The kid?" Jacob said. "No way in hell. Without us, he's nothing."

"Well," Pooch said, "he was the only one of us who could sweet-talk those old gals."

"He was getting too uppity."

"I'm not arguing. Just saying. When are we getting rid of that stuff, anyway?"

"Tomorrow. Meeting a guy in town."

"Hey, girls," Stevie said. "Come on over here and get some of this."

2

TRAVELING MONEY

When Paul woke, it was 2:00 p.m. He was so stiff he had to roll off the bed to get to his feet. He undressed, leaving his dirty clothes on the floor, went into the bathroom, and looked in the mirror. The bruise at his hairline looked a little better. There were two heel-shaped bruises on his ribs, and a number of small bruises scattered across his stomach. He couldn't lift his right arm over his head. He took a shower, first hot, then cold, staying in as long as he could stand it. Then he put on clean clothes.

He sat on the edge of the bed, looking at the phone as if he expected it to tell him what to do. Finally, he looked in the phone book for the number of Speedy Joe's Subs and More, ordered a twelve-inch Italian sub and a large Coke delivered, and lay down. There was a knock on the door. He paid the delivery girl, sat back down on the bed, ate the sub, drank the Coke, and went back to sleep. When he woke up, it was two hours later. Now was the time to get out of town.

He opened his suitcase on the bed and checked it. It was already packed to go. He needed to start working smarter, and he needed better partners. If Jacob, Stevie, and Pooch hadn't been involved, he could have lived off Cicilie for six months, filled his pockets, and she wouldn't have cared. Hell, she would have begged him to stay. But even that was too much risk. Her friends cared about her too much. And an innocent person—a person with nothing to hide—could always go to the police. No, the ideal mark was one who wouldn't call the police—who didn't want anyone to know what had happened because they were guilty of something. Those were the kind of marks he needed to find. But what to do now? Two hundred dollars wasn't going to carry him far enough to get something else started. How much counterfeit could he get for that? Two thousand? Jacob's counterfeiter was in Pikesville. He'd have to drive all day, but it would be worth it. It was as good a place to start as any.

He dug down in his suitcase to find his ring of shanked car keys. They'd proven to be a good investment. They would open and start most cars, which meant he could drive a stolen car without attracting suspicion. Out in the parking lot, an old Honda Civic was parked away from the building. He found the Civic key on the ring, slid it in the door lock, and jiggled it as he turned it. The door lock popped. He put his suitcase in the back seat. The Civic started on the first turn of the key. It was full of gas. Maybe his luck was changing.

The following afternoon, Paul arrived in Pikesville. He left the Honda in the downtown bus station parking lot, rented a locker for his suitcase, and took a cab to the High Five Tavern. A group of retired men sat at one of the Formica-topped tables, playing cards and nursing beers. The bartender, a black man with a short Afro and a toothpick hanging from his lips, turned from the TV behind the long walnut bar. "What can I get you?"

"I'm looking for Stella."

The bartender stepped out from behind the bar and cracked open a door at the back marked Private. "Someone to see you," he said.

Stella came into the barroom. She was a handsome, dark-haired woman wearing tight jeans, high-heeled boots, and a sleeveless top. "You're one of Jacob's guys."

"Not any more."

"Good for you. Come on into the back."

All three of them went into the back room. Boxes of liquor and cases of beer were stacked up against the back wall. A gray, government-surplus desk sat to one side. The back door had an iron bar padlocked across it. "Check him over, Gary."

The bartender patted Paul down, took his .38, and handed it to Stella. "Why are you here?" she asked.

"I need to buy some paper."

"How much?"

"How much can I get for one hundred sixty dollars?"

"I usually don't deal in petty cash."

"I understand. I'm just trying to get to a place where I can get on my feet."

"You're pretty banged up. Jacob push you out?"

"Yeah."

"For cause?"

"Difference of opinion."

"Tell you what; are you in a hurry?"

He shrugged.

"You do me a favor, and I'll take care of you."

He looked her up and down appraisingly. "What kind of favor?"

She laughed. "You're pretty enough, but it's not that kind of favor."

"As long as it doesn't involve killing."

"You won't kill anyone?"

"Not if I don't have to."

"There's a guy I want you to follow. He knows my guys. I want to know everywhere he goes and everyone he sees."

"How long?"

"Three days should do it."

"I don't have a car or any ID."

"You are one lost puppy, aren't you? Gary will hook you up and give you all the details." She handed back his gun.

THREE DAYS LATER, Paul returned to the back room of the High Five Tavern.

"What have you got for me?" Stella asked.

"Everything you asked." He set a camera and manila envelope down on the government surplus desk.

"Twenty-four seven?"

"Absolutely. I slept in the car."

"Go over it."

He pulled a stack of photos out of the envelope. The top photo showed a small, white, clapboard house with a porch swing. A dark-haired man in a blue suit was standing on the porch. The next photo showed the man and a black woman in a bathrobe. "That's your guy. He was there all three days at different times of the day. Sometimes he was carrying a bag, sometimes he wasn't."

The third photo showed a bar. "He also went here every day at five."

"Curley's?" Stella asked.

"Yeah. There's a card game in the back. Couldn't get a picture there."

The fourth photo showed a two-story brick house in an upscale neighborhood. The fifth picture showed two blond children, a boy and a girl, playing in the yard. The sixth picture showed a good-looking blonde woman in yoga clothes getting out of a blue minivan. "This is where he spent all three nights. Otherwise, he was just running errands, eating in restaurants—normal stuff. Except when he was here, of course. I took a bunch of other pictures just in case. They're all in the envelope."

Stella pushed the photos into a pile. A tear started down her cheek. "You haven't asked me what this is all about."

"That's because it's none of my business."

"The driver's license and Social Security card we gave you are top quality. They should more than pay for the job."

"They aren't in my name."

"You don't like being Roy Stevens? You need to stop using your birth name. Someday it might be valuable to you."

"You said you'd take care of me."

"I remember." She reached into the top drawer of the desk.

"Here's five thousand counterfeit. I'm going to mark you down for five hundred."

"I really appreciate it. I'll pay you back as soon as I can."

"Where you going?"

"I don't know."

"Just a traveling man, huh? Well, don't be a stranger. I may have another job for you sometime."

Paul walked out of the tavern and into the afternoon glare. Stella was a good person to know. He needed more friends like her. And the job? That was the easiest work he'd done in a long time. He went into a Stop-N-Go and used the pay phone to call a cab. From there he went to the convention center downtown.

Happy hour was in full swing at the convention center bar. A crowd of men and women in business clothes with conference nametags clipped onto their jackets were networking with acquaintances and catching up with old friends. Paul bumped into a man who was leaving the bar and lifted his name tag. Now he was Jeremy Singer. He circled the room, on the lookout for a particular type of woman: middle-aged, married, expensive clothes, drinking alone. A woman whose dress and makeup showed that she considered herself sexually desirable. Preferably a woman whose nametag indicated that she was at a different conference than Jeremy Singer. He went to the bar, ordered a beer, and paid for it with a counterfeit twenty. Then he sat down at a table in the far corner with a good view of the space and waited.

There were a couple of likely candidates, but it was too soon to move. It was best if they got enough drinks in them to begin to feel lonely. Groups were leaving for dinner. The bar was beginning to empty out. Two women came up to one of his prospects. She immediately brightened up, and they all left together. Another of his prospects asked for a bar phone, made a call, and turned down the bartender's inquiry about another drink.

But his third prospect was hard drinking, hunched down on her stool like she was never leaving. She was slim, with dark, shoulder-length hair. She wore an ivory suit. A wedding ring that glittered with diamonds was on her left hand, and a gold bracelet was on her right wrist. The perfunctory strand of pearls hung around her neck. Paul waited until the bartender was in close proximity to her. Then he went up to the bar next to her and flagged the bartender. "Another beer, please."

The bartender nodded. Paul glanced at the woman. Her name tag read Sandra Malone. "Hi," he said.

"Hi."

The bartender set his beer in front of him.

"Which conference you at?"

She gave him a puzzled look.

"I'm sorry. Just making conversation."

She smiled. "No, no, I was just thinking about something else."

"I'm Jeremy. I'm at the pharmaceutical meetings."

"I'm Sandy. Insurance Alliance."

"I've seen a lot of your name tags around."

She glanced down at her name tag. "I should take this off. Today was our last day."

"Your friends already gone?"

"Yeah."

He smiled. Her eyes were bloodshot. She was already slurring her words. This was going to be so easy. "So you've been here all week? You must know where all the good restaurants are."

Later, up in the hallway in front of the door to her hotel room, she grabbed his ass while he unlocked the door. He hoped she was blackout drunk. "You're a naughty girl."

She giggled. She put her arms around him and kissed him. They stumbled into the dark room. The moonlight fell in through the open drapes. He pushed the door shut with his foot. She started tugging at his clothes. "What's your hurry?" he asked. "We've got all night."

He helped her out of her jacket and skirt and led her to the bed. "I'm married," she said.

"I know."

"I don't do this very often."

"I don't care."

They both laughed.

She took off her blouse and lay down on the bed in her bra and panties, watching him. He pulled off his clothes and laid them over a chair. "God, you're perfect," she said.

He climbed up onto the bed. "You're drunk."

She laid her head back on the pillow. He finished undressing her. She started to speak, but he closed her mouth with a kiss.

When they were finished, she fell asleep curled up beside him. He listened for a while to the rhythm of her breathing before he slowly rolled off the bed. He stood watching her in the moonlight while he dressed. No movement. He fished her wallet out of her handbag, stepped into the bathroom, and turned on the light. One hundred and eighty dollars, cash. He left her with a maid tip and cab fare to the airport. No need to be mean. Then he looked through her credit cards, thumbing past the ones that were the easiest to take out. Back by her health insurance card was a MasterCard in her husband's name. This was the jackpot. Why was she carrying it? It would be days—maybe even weeks—before she missed it.

He turned off the bathroom light, crept back across the room to replace her wallet, and then stood watching her for a few more minutes. It seemed like she'd had a good time. It was a shame she probably wouldn't remember it. Maybe this would be her wake-up call to deal with her drinking problem. He cracked the door open just wide enough to slip out, heard it click shut, and pushed it to make sure it was properly closed. It was 2:30 a.m.

3

LOOKING FOR PARTNERS

Four months later, Paul, now going by the name Roy Stevens, was sitting in his sky-blue Cadillac in a Subway parking lot, eating a tuna sub and thinking about his next move. He'd arrived in Fredericksburg, the city where Pooch lived when he wasn't on a job with Jacob and Stevie, a week ago. Roy wanted to know the when and where of their next job so he could rip them off and screw them over. They'd cheated him and tried to get him killed. They owed him money. Now he was going to get even. Pooch was a talker. Liked to talk. Liked to make friends. So he was the most likely candidate to give up the information Roy needed. But he wasn't going to give the information to Roy, so Roy needed partners that Pooch didn't know. He'd reached out to a few grifters that he knew were reliable, but thus far no one was interested in partnering on a job that was more personal than business.

Across Kennedy Boulevard Roy saw a couple walking down the sidewalk. The woman—just a kid, really—was a knockout. She was movie-star pretty, and she knew it. Her dark hair was braided down her back, and she was wearing a tiny summer dress that fluttered in the breeze. All her movements said naïve waif, but—it really did take one to know one, didn't it? The shift of her hip as she walked, the way her braid swayed—Roy was willing to bet she was a born player.

The guy who was following her, maybe a couple of years older than her, looked like a former high school football player. He wore shorts, flip-flops, and a Hawaiian shirt. He had that self-satisfied look on his face that some guys have when they know that the woman they're with is way out of their league, and thus the entire world has misjudged their value. Roy chuckled. That guy probably thought he was in charge. She had to be on the con, but was he a con artist or just muscle? Roy was willing to bet that he loved her, but did she love him? Or was he just her meal ticket?

The girl stepped over to the curb and stuck out her thumb. Jail-bait. Here was the test. No one who could see who she really was would pull over to give them a ride. A bald guy in a red Audi put on his flashers and pulled over. She got in the front, and her boy got in the back. What was their game? Roy pulled out of the Subway parking lot and followed them. The Audi rolled through three traffic lights before it turned into a city park. What was she telling him? That her boy would go for a walk while they did some business?

The Audi pulled into a parking spot by a picnic table under a huge shade tree. Roy pulled over to the side of the road by a park bench. The driver's door on the Audi popped open and the bald guy fell out. He started to get up. He was yelling something. The boy came out the door after him, leaned down to punch him in the face, and then kicked at him. The man scrambled away on his hands and knees. The boy climbed back into the Audi and drove away, leaving the bald guy yelling and shaking his fist.

Roy followed the Audi into the industrial part of town, where it pulled into Whitehead's Auto Salvage. He smiled. Stealing cars from lechers and selling them to a chop shop. How long did they think they could get away with that? A few minutes later, the girl and boy left the salvage yard in a white Dodge Dakota driven by an unshaven kid wearing a ball cap. Roy followed them to a trailer park situated behind a discount strip mall anchored by a Kmart. The truck stopped in front of a dilapidated singlewide trailer with a rusty white AMC

Spirit parked in front. Roy pulled to the curb. The girl kissed the driver before she and her boy got out of the truck. The boy unlocked the trailer, and they went inside. Were they done for the day? Roy drove past the trailer, turned around, and parked under a tree with a good view of the trailer's door.

At about five o'clock, they came out of the trailer and got into the rusty Spirit. She was still wearing her tiny frock. Her boy had changed into a black T-shirt, black jeans, and work boots. He climbed into the driver's seat. Roy followed them across town to Juanita's, a tequila bar located in a shopping area next to a cluster of hotels. The Spirit pulled into the side lot and parked with a view of the entrance. Roy parked his Cadillac on the street where he could see the parking lot and the front door. The girl went into the bar. The boy stayed in the car.

Roy gave the girl a few minutes to get her game underway before he went in. The place was busy. Tex-Mex music blared from the speakers. Servers in white tops and short black skirts moved among the tables. The bartenders were all dark-haired men wearing white shirts and cowboy belts with large buckles. The clientele were mainly men, many of whom seemed to be pounding down shots. He spotted the girl standing with three thirty-something businessmen at the bar. She had her repartee down: the smile, the eye contact, the touch on the arm, the disarming giggle. She didn't have any trouble working all three of those guys at the same time. But what was the game? Picking pockets? Prostitution? Something bigger? Why did she need the boy in the parking lot? Roy elbowed his way up to the bar at a spot where he could keep an eye on her and ordered a beer. He felt a touch on his arm. A blonde, an old twenty-two-year-old wearing a frilly party dress that showed a lot of cleavage, smiled up at him.

"Looking for some company?"

He leaned down to whisper in her ear. "I'm busy, but you can use me for camouflage until you spot your mark."

"What kind of game you in?" she asked.

He shrugged. "Buy you a drink?"

Twenty minutes later, his date spotted a drunk she liked on the other side of the bar. "Be seeing you," she said.

Roy turned his attention back to his girl. The three guys with her were getting progressively drunker, but she wasn't. She was faking it. Easy to tell if you're sober—not so easy if you're loaded. They ordered another round of shots. That's when he noticed that the bartender was pouring hers from a different bottle than the guys. Very smooth.

Finally, things were beginning to sort themselves out. One guy was getting most of her attention; the others were turning into wingmen. The chosen guy was beginning to get that hungry look in his eye. He put his hands on her hips. She smiled and patted his hands before she moved them away. Then she glanced around as if she were afraid of making a scene. She grabbed his tie and pulled his face down to hers so that she could whisper in his ear. Then she left. The guy said something to his buddies. One of them slapped him on the back. The guy set his face to try to convince the world that he wasn't drunk and followed her.

Roy slipped out the door behind the lucky winner. He and the girl were in the parking lot in the shadows by the building, kissing and groping. He had her skirt up and his hand in her panties. Her boy came out of the Spirit, moving fast. Roy ducked down behind a car to watch. Her boy grabbed the business guy, pushed him back to the wall as she feigned surprise, gut-punched him twice, and took his wallet from his back pocket while he threw up on his shoes. The girl ran as if she were afraid. Her boy took the cash from the business guy's wallet, tossed the wallet on the ground, ran back to the Spirit, and drove off.

Roy jogged to the curb, where he saw the Spirit pull over to pick up the girl. It was a well-oiled machine. Maybe these two could help him get the information he needed from Pooch. He hurried back to the business guy. "Hey, buddy, you okay?"

The guy was picking up his wallet. "Did you see that?"

"That was crazy. Who was that guy?"

"I don't know. I don't know what happened."

"Were you in the bar? You got any friends around here?"

"Yeah, I was right in here."

"Let's go back inside."

THE NEXT MORNING, Roy was back watching the door to their trailer. They surfaced a little after eleven and walked over to the Gas-N-Go on the corner of the strip mall. Roy followed them in. She kept the counter guy busy with her easy banter and exposed cleavage while her boy worked the aisles, filling his pockets and shoving a package of rolls under his shirt before he slipped out the door. She bought two small coffees. They met at the bus stop, where they sat on the bench to enjoy their breakfast. Shoplifting, rolling drunks, and carjacking seemed to be their stock in trade. She was the grifter, and he was the muscle—that much was certain. They were doing the best they could do together, but with a little direction she could be doing a lot better. She had the magic. She'd walked that guy at Juanita's into a mugging without even breaking a sweat. So why was she carrying her boy? Was it lack of confidence? Lack of imagination? True love? Roy got back in his Cadillac. It was time to get to know them.

They strolled down to Kennedy Boulevard again. The traffic was busy. Were they really going to try to jack another car? She stepped to the curb and stuck out her thumb. Roy smiled. He made the turn onto the boulevard and pulled up to her. "How far you going?"

She smiled. "All the way down to Patrick Avenue."

"Hop in."

She sprawled across the front seat, legs spread, her dress just covering her panties. "Hot day," she said.

Her boy got in the back. "Thanks, mister."

Roy pulled away from the curb. "What's your name?"

"I'm Candy, and he's Joe."

"I bet. Let me ask you a question, Candy."

She touched his shoulder. "You're not shy, are you?"

"No, I'm not."

She batted her eyes. "What you got in mind?"

"No disrespect. I'm not judging. I was just wondering how many days in a row you think you can pull the same stunt?"

"What are you talking about?"

"Don't get me wrong. It was fun to watch. Could you see the look on that guy's face when your boy pitched him out of his Audi?"

She closed her legs and sat up straight. "Who are you? You're not a cop."

"No, a cop would have waited for you to offer your ass for cash. What did the salvage yard give you for a car that hot? Couple a hundred?"

Her boy leaned up in the back seat. "Let us out."

"We're going to talk first. You two do anything besides hijack cars, roll drunks, and shoplift?"

Her boy smacked the back of Roy's seat. "Stop the car before I bust your head."

"You touch me, and I step on the gas. I'm in the safest crash spot in this car."

He could feel her watching him. "What do you want?" she said. "We don't have any money."

"That was some good work in the bar last night. The bartender was pouring you water. Was that his play or management's?"

She didn't say anything.

"I was wondering if you wanted to step up your game. Make more money."

"Who the hell are you?"

"You can call me the Traveling Man."

"What kind of name is that?"

"It's a name—like Candy or Joe."

"Okay, Traveling Man, what you got in mind?"

"Maybe we call your bluff," her boy said. "Fuck you up and take your ride."

"Relax, baby. Let's hear what the man has to say."

"There's a crew I want to rip off," Roy said. "Your end would be three, four thousand, at least."

"What kind of crew?"

"Robbery gang. They always party after they finish a job. We swoop in and take their score while they're passed out."

"And what would we do?"

"You'd play your usual roles, but you might have to stretch a little."

"I don't like it," her boy said.

"Sounds like it's dangerous," she said.

"Not if it's done right. Look, I'm offering you two a chance to move up in the world. The door is open, you just got to walk through."

She looked back at her boy. "What do you think?"

Roy glanced in the rearview mirror. The boy was shaking his head. "Sorry," she said. "Thanks for the offer, but we have to pass."

"Where do you want me to drop you off?"

"Right here would be fine."

Roy put on his flashers and pulled over. She was interested, but her boy was wary. Maybe he was jealous. Afraid he'd lose her. Liked thinking he was in charge. But Roy didn't need him. Muscle you could pick up anywhere. She, on the other hand, had talent that could be developed. The two of them grifting together could be something special. So maybe what he needed to do was separate them long enough for her to choose to come with him.

Carol and Terry watched the Cadillac disappear around the corner. "What's next?" she asked.

"Try for another sucker," Terry said.

"Maybe that guy was right. Maybe we should space them out."

"The first of the month is coming up. We still don't have enough money to pay all our bills."

"We could have gone in with him."

"I don't trust him." He gripped her hand.

"Don't be jealous."

"I'm not jealous."

"Admit it. He's a charmer, like me, and you're afraid he's going to charm my panties off."

Terry twisted her wrist. "I'm not jealous. I just don't trust him."

She grimaced. "Baby, you're my guy. Only you. You've got nothing to be afraid of. I said no."

"Okay, then." He let go of her hand.

She rubbed her wrist. "So what's it going to be?"

"Let's try for another one."

"Okay." She stepped to the curb and put out her thumb.

OVER THE NEXT FEW DAYS, Roy shadowed them. Their MO remained the same. In the afternoon they'd flag down a car. Sometimes they'd steal it; sometimes they'd just rob the driver. For happy hour, they'd work a bar frequented by tourists or businessmen. The girl would lure the mark outside, and her boy would rob him. Afterward, they partied, which explained why they were living in a dump. It was a simple, effective program that was bound to land them in jail sooner rather than later. But the more Roy watched her work, the more convinced he was that she would make an excellent partner if he could win her over.

At 7:00 p.m., Roy stood at a pay phone on the street a few storefronts down from Casper's Bar and Grill. The girl was inside, and her boy was sitting in the Spirit in the parking lot. The door to the bar opened. The girl, clad in her usual tiny dress, and a big guy in a tan suit spilled out onto the street holding hands and turned into the parking lot. It looked as if suit guy was trying to guide her to his car while she was kissing him and stumbling along. Roy dialed 911. "There's a fight in the parking lot at Casper's Bar and Grill. Hurry."

Roy kept his head down as he crossed the street to his Cadillac. Her boy rushed across the parking lot, pushed suit guy away from her, and punched him. But this guy didn't fold up. He slipped into a boxer's stance, chin down, one leg forward, and jabbed her boy twice in the face. The girl squealed. Her boy shook off the blows, and the fight was on.

Roy smiled. What a lucky break. This time the cops were certain to get here in time. Suit guy and her boy were banging off the parked cars like the main event on All Star Wrestling when two police cruisers rolled up. The girl ran. One of the cops ordered them to stop fighting. Suit guy stepped back and lowered his arms, but her boy kept swinging. The nearest cop Tased him. He crumpled to the pavement. Then the cop handcuffed him behind his back. The other cop took a statement from suit guy. A few bystanders started watching from the sidewalk. Her boy struggled and yelled while the cops loaded him into the back of one of the cruisers. Suit guy got in his car and left. Roy sat in his Cadillac watching the parking lot until the girl finally came back for the Spirit. Then he followed her back to the trailer park. So far, so good.

CAROL TOSSED the car keys onto the kitchen table in the trailer and sat on the worn-out sofa. Was Terry going to blame her? That guy hadn't seemed like a tough guy. He was wearing a suit, for Christ's sake. And he drank as much as any of them. But now the cops had Terry. She walked back through the kitchen, where dirty dishes were piled in the sink, to the bedroom, where Terry's side of the unmade bed looked just as it had when he rolled out this morning. What would she do without him? She'd never actually fucked anyone for money. Flirting with guys, kissing them and letting them feel her up, manipulating them, knowing that she was safe, that no one was going to hurt her—sure, she'd been smacked a couple of times, but then Terry paid them back. She sat down on Terry's side of the bed, held his pillow to her chest, and smelled it. What was she going to do?

She didn't know how long she'd been sitting there when the phone rang. She ran through to the living room to pick it up.

"Hey, Carol."

She smiled. "Terry, are you okay?"

"I'm at the jail. I'll see the judge in the morning. Maybe I'll be able to get this misunderstanding cleared up. As soon as I know what's going on, I'll call. So stay near the phone."

"I don't know what happened. I'm so sorry."

"Not now. I'll call tomorrow."

"I'll be waiting. I love you."

"I love you, too."

She hung up the phone. The trailer seemed too quiet. She double-checked the front and back doors to make sure they were locked, and then turned on all the lights. She felt empty and afraid. Whenever she slept alone, nightmares plagued her. She didn't know how she was going to go to sleep without Terry there beside her. She turned on the TV, just for the background noise, and walked back through to the bedroom. There was half a fifth of Early Times whiskey on the dresser. She took a slug, felt the heat explode in her belly, and took another slug. Then she lay down in her clothes. She felt under the bed to make sure she could reach the claw hammer she kept there. She closed her eyes and tried to control her breathing. It was going to be a long night.

She tossed and turned until she finally fell asleep at 3:00 a.m. The neighbor's door slamming at 7:30 woke her. She lay in bed for another hour, but she couldn't go back to sleep. She showered, put on Daisy Dukes and a pink T-shirt, and peeked out the window. It looked like it was going to be a pretty day, but she felt foggy, as if she were in a bizarre dream. She looked in the refrigerator, found a can of iced tea, and made a peanut butter and jelly sandwich for breakfast. It was 9:15. The phone hadn't rung. There was some morning talk show on the TV. The hosts seemed way too happy.

She took all the dirty dishes out of the sink, ran the sink full of soapy water, washed all the dishes, and wiped down the counters. Ten a.m. Finally, the phone rang.

"Hey, Carol."

"Terry. How did it go? When do I come get you?"

"Listen. They charged me with assault and battery."

"What does that mean?"

"It means six months in jail."

"Six months? You couldn't get out of it?"

"The cops claimed it was attempted robbery to begin with—they had that guy's statement. I didn't have a record, so the judge said assault and battery—two thousand dollars or six months. We don't have the money. It sucks, but that's the way it is. Don't worry about me. I'll be fine. I'll probably get out earlier."

"When can I see you?"

"You don't want to come around here for a while. The cop said I had a woman accomplice. Maybe there was a surveillance camera in that parking lot. I don't know. I didn't see one. So give it a few days."

"Call me."

"I will."

"I'm going to get that money."

"I don't know how."

"Don't be mad at me."

He didn't reply.

"I love you," she said.

"I love you, too."

Carol hung up the phone. What could she do? She had about $150 in her wallet, and there was another $600 in the shoebox where they kept their savings. Seven-fifty total. Rent and bills at the first of the month would empty the shoebox. Every day she needed food money and gas for the car. She couldn't shoplift every meal. And she'd never actually done the shoplifting. She'd provided the distraction so that Terry could do it. Her skills were useless without him. She couldn't work their scam by herself. She couldn't lure a man to a quiet location and force him to give her his money. The force was Terry's job. And even if she offered sex for money—even if her situation were that desperate—she wouldn't make half of what they made robbing Johns. She'd still need a waitress job. And she'd be no closer to raising the two thousand than she was now.

She went back into the bedroom, pulled her T-shirt off over her head, and kicked off her Daisy Dukes. The man in the blue Cadillac —the Traveling Man—had said they could make three or four thousand dollars partnering with him. She put on sexy underwear and a clean summer dress. Maybe that guy was still around. Maybe he still needed help. Maybe she could charm him into fronting her the money to get Terry out of jail. Maybe if she could get Terry out of jail quickly enough, he wouldn't be too angry with her.

4

CAROL

Roy was sitting in a window booth at the Cup-N-Sup diner at the strip mall in front of the girl's trailer park. His car was parked right in front of the building. He'd eaten the Iron Man breakfast—three eggs, pancakes, sausage, and hash browns —and was sipping his third cup of coffee while he read the newspaper. He was fairly certain that her boy was locked up, which meant that the girl needed his help. As soon as she figured that out, she would be looking for him, so all he had to do was make sure that he would be in her way.

After he finished the metro section, he glanced out the window. And there she was, in her waif persona, walking across the parking lot toward his car. He left a tip on the table and took his check up to the counter. She was posing against his car like a model in a magazine when he came out of the diner.

"Hey," he said.

She smiled. "How are you?"

"I'm good. To what do I owe this pleasure?"

"I've had some time to think about your offer."

"Really?" He glanced around. "Where's your boy?"

"Is the offer still open?"

He nodded. "Yes, it is."

"Then we're in. But I need a favor."

"I'm listening."

"We're going to make three or four thousand for our end on this job?"

"Absolutely. At least."

"I need two thousand to get Terry out of jail."

"So Terry is your boy's real name?"

She nodded.

"Let me guess. Terry got picked up on an assault charge."

"Yeah."

"I'm not going to front you that kind of money."

"He can't help if he's in jail."

"I don't need his help that bad."

"I need him out of jail."

"Look, I don't know you that well. You help me with the job, you get paid. You can hire a lawyer to try to get your boy out if he hasn't been released. Everybody wins."

"You don't understand."

"I do understand. He's your man. You need him. But he's not my man."

She started to walk away.

He called after her. "Think about it. It's the best offer you're going to get."

She turned back toward him. "I can't run my game without him. How do I get money to live on until we pull your job?"

"Are you in my crew? 'Cause if you're in my crew, I take care of you."

"You take care of me?" She put her hand on her hip. "In exchange for what?"

"In exchange for your expertise. Get in the car. We'll talk about it."

She stood there looking at him.

"Really. Get in the car."

They sat down in the Cadillac. He turned toward her and put his arm up on the back of the seat. "Right now, you live hand-to-mouth. Am I right?"

She shrugged.

"That's over with. You don't have bills to pay anymore. We collect your gear, and you come stay at my apartment. This is strictly business. When we make the score, all the expenses come off the top then we split what's left. I take fifty percent. If it's just the two of us, you take the other half. Then we decide if we continue together. You can hook back up with Terry when he gets out. That's your business. Does that seem fair?"

"If you keep your word."

"And that's what you need Terry for? For protection?"

"Yes."

"What's your name?"

"You know my name."

"I mean your real name, not the *nom de guerre* that goes with the tiny dress and the carefully played innocence."

"Carol."

"Okay, Carol. It's a pretty good act you got going, but you're not fooling me. So you can cut the bullshit when it's just us. When you work with me, I won't hit you or threaten you or lie to you. If I yell at you, it's not personal. It's to get a reaction from someone else. What I need from you is to always tell me the truth. Do we understand each other?"

"Yes."

"So we're partners?" He stuck out his right hand.

"What's your name?"

"Roy Stevens."

"Okay, Roy." She shook his hand.

"Let's go get your stuff."

She started to give him directions, but he waved her off. "I know where you live."

"How?"

"I've been following you. How do you think I knew about the carjacking and Juanita's?" He shrugged. "I told you I wouldn't lie."

He drove to the trailer park and parked in front of her trailer behind the Spirit. She sat in the Cadillac for a moment looking out the windshield; then she gave him a significant look.

"Yeah," he said, "I know. It's the point of no return. You've got to trust me or run me off."

"If you hurt me, I'll get even."

"I believe you. But I'm not going to hurt you. I need you on my team. I've got to trust you, and you've got to trust me. Okay?"

"Okay."

She got out of the car. He followed her into the trailer. The sofa, TV, and kitchen table were the kind of worn-out you only ever saw in a place that came fully furnished. "What do you need to pack?"

"Our clothes, some odds and ends."

He sat on the sofa. She got a box of garbage bags from under the kitchen sink, took it into the bedroom, and folded their clothes into the garbage bags, hers and Terry's. Then she stripped the bed, shoving the sheets, blankets, and pillows into more bags. She brought five bags to the front door. "Should I bring any stuff out of the refrigerator?"

"No need."

She went back into the bedroom, found a cardboard box in the closet, put the Early Times whiskey in it, and went into the bathroom for the toiletries and her makeup. She put their savings shoebox on top, covered everything with the bath towels, and carried the box out to the living room. "I think that's it. Help me carry this stuff out to my car."

They put the bags and the box into the trunk of the Spirit.

"We done here?" he asked.

"Let me take one more look around."

She walked through the trailer, looking everything over. It was their home—hers and Terry's. It was the place they had set up house when they'd quit living in his car, after she'd found him and found out that he'd do whatever she wanted as long as he thought it was his idea. He was a good boyfriend. Rarely hit her, even when she deserved it. Always shared any food, or drink, or cash. Always took her side in a fight. If they had to run, he always let her run first. He did have a jealous streak, but he was her man, and she was going to do whatever it took to get him out of jail. She owed him that.

Roy's APARTMENT was a two-bedroom in a lower-middle-class apartment complex near a shopping mall that was on its last legs. Older cars filled the parking lot. Children, many unsupervised, rushed around in the fenced-off playground. Roy and Carol pulled into the two spots in front of Roy's door. He helped her carry her bags in.

"Up the stairs," he said.

They went up the stairs and down the hall to an empty room with a stripped bed in it. Roy set down the bags he was carrying. "This is your room. I'm next door. The bathroom is at the end of the hall. Make yourself at home."

Carol hung up her clothes, but she left Terry's in the bags. Then she made the bed and took her toiletries and towel down to the bathroom. Roy's towel and shaving kit hung from one of the towel racks. She put her makeup bag on top of the toilet tank, her shampoo on the shower shelf, and her towel on the other towel rack. She brought the box back to her room, set it upside down next to the bed for a night table, and put the Early Times bottle on it.

When she got downstairs, Roy was standing in the living room, looking out the window. "All set?"

She nodded.

"Here's a door key."

She took the key and put it in her handbag.

He looked her over. "Is that the way you always dress?"

"More or less."

"Sometimes you'll need to make some changes so that you blend in rather than stand out. Do you have clothes so that you can do that?"

She looked at his dress pants and sports coat. "You mean so that I sort of match you?"

He nodded.

She shook her head.

"Have you eaten?"

"No."

"Let's get some lunch. Then we'll go shopping."

"Are you serious?"

"We've got to get in some practice together—get a feel for each other's rhythm so that we don't trip each other up. Every job requires the right clothes."

"Okay, it's your game."

"What kind of food do you like?"

By HAPPY HOUR, they were sitting in a booth in the dimly lit Summertown Grill, a bar and grill located near an office complex. Instead of her tiny sundress, Carol was now wearing a shirtdress that a clerical worker might wear. The area along the stainless steel bar was crowded with men and women dressed as if they'd come from the office. The conversation competed with the contemporary pop music wafting in through the speaker system.

"Okay," Roy said. "In a place like this, you're used to charming a guy for Terry to mug, so I'm going to guess that you don't pickpocket."

"What's the point?"

"It's the same money as a mugging, only you don't need somebody waiting in the parking lot."

"Unless something goes wrong."

"Nothing goes wrong if you know how. The next hour is prime time. It's more difficult when the crowd thins out. Look around the room. Where are the best spots?"

She glanced around for a moment. "Over by the servers' station at the bar. There's a knot of people pushing into one another whenever the server shows up."

"Good. Where else?"

"Where people are leaving the restrooms, if someone is standing behind a person on a barstool, trying to flag the bartender, they jostle into them."

"A little tougher, but still good." Roy smiled. "Open handbags and wallets in jacket pockets are the easiest. In this room, you've got the advantage."

"How have I got the advantage?"

"Women are less skittish about being bumped into by a woman, and if a man feels your hand going for his back pocket, you can always flirt. I'll go first. Watch me."

Roy slid out of the booth. He weaved through the crowd along the bar, noting couples and groups, tight places between them, open handbags, and bulges in jacket pockets. He pushed through the door to the men's room, ignored the line, and washed his hands. As he came out of the men's room, he fell in step behind a curvy blonde carrying a large bag on a shoulder strap. The bag was open. As she shifted to move around two men, he brushed by her on the other side, "Excuse me, honey," palmed her wallet, and slipped it into his sports coat pocket.

He sat back down in the booth, flashed the wallet at Carol, and slipped it back into his pocket. "Now I'm going to give it back."

"Why?"

"If she notices it's gone and makes a fuss, you won't get your chance."

He made his way up into the crowd at the bar, where he found the blonde talking with two girlfriends. He bent down and came up with the wallet in his hand. "Excuse me," he said. "I think you dropped this."

The blonde looked at him, looked at the wallet, and shoved her hand into her bag. "My gosh. It is mine."

"If you could check inside, show me a picture ID, just to be sure—"

She flipped out her driver's license.

"That's not a bad likeness for the DMV."

She put her license back in her wallet and shoved her wallet down into her bag. "Thanks so much."

"Don't mention it."

He made his way back to the booth. "Now it's your turn. Remember, you're not trying to attract attention to yourself. If you get caught in the act, revert to what you know. Guys are putty in your hands. If things go bad, break off as quickly as you can and go outside."

"Why?"

"You want to avoid a scene. People have to rubberneck. Then someone remembers what you look like. That's bad for us. So if there's trouble, go outside. I'll come to you."

She started to slide out of the booth. He pointed toward her throat. "Unbutton the top button. It's happy hour."

She walked up to the edge of the crowd by the bar and leaned against a pillar. How to decide? The crush by the servers' station seemed best. There appeared to be two groups there: a man and a woman closest to the servers' station, and three men next to them who appeared to be drunk. When one of the servers wasn't there, they expanded into her station. When a server showed up, they bunched up out of her way, the men pushing together as the woman moved over. The sweet spot would be to take the guy's wallet as the woman pushed against him. She looked for the servers out among the tables. A woman was approaching with a tray of dirty glasses. She crossed in front of Carol. Carol stepped into her wake.

Just as the couple pulled away from the servers' station, Carol pushed in on the other side of the guy they were pushing into. It was like everything was happening in slow motion. His hips shifted. She got her thumb and two fingers on his wallet. She palmed it and slipped it into the pocket on her dress. Then she stuck up her hand for the bartender. Her heart was pounding like crazy.

"Just a second," the bartender said.

The guy she'd pickpocketed looked down at her. "Hey, gorgeous. Where did you come from?"

She gave him a dismissive look.

"How about if I buy you a drink?"

His two friends on the other side of her chimed in. "You by yourself?" one said.

"You shouldn't drink alone," the other one said.

"I'm buying my own drinks."

"Don't be like that." The guy put his hand on her shoulder.

"Take your hand off me."

"Whoa, no disrespect." He held his hands up. His friends sniggered.

She turned and walked away as if she were in a huff. When she was clear of the bar crowd, she crossed back to the booth.

"How did it feel?" Roy asked.

"A little shaky at first, but then I fell into character."

"What did I tell you? Easy as pie. How much did you get?"

She opened the wallet. "About sixty bucks and a credit card," she said without looking up.

"Do you like coming here?"

"Yeah, sure."

"Do you want to make it our regular place for while we're in town?"

She shrugged.

He smiled. "Then you have to give the wallet back."

"With the money?"

He nodded.

"That guy was an asshole."

"Doesn't matter. Never work where you play. It'll always come back to bite you."

"I don't want to talk to that guy again."

"Find another way."

She scooted out of the booth and walked back to the pillar at the edge of the bar crowd. A server was waiting at the servers' station. Just as she started to pick up her tray, Carol stepped forward and dropped the wallet at the guy's feet. Then she turned to the server. "Looks like that guy dropped his wallet."

"Why don't you tell him?"

"He was pestering me a minute ago. I don't want to encourage him."

She rolled her eyes and nodded. She stepped over to the guys. Carol walked away.

When she got back to the booth, Roy was signing a credit card slip. "What's up?" she asked.

"We're done here. Let's go to dinner."

BACK AT THE APARTMENT, just before Roy was about to go to sleep, he was sitting up in bed with the night table lamp on, thinking about Carol's first day. She was definitely game to try new tricks—she was a natural pickpocket—and she didn't get flustered, but he hadn't really taken her out of her element yet. With straight men, she could default to flirting whenever she wanted. How would she work a straight woman? Or a lesbian, for that matter? What sort of little scam could they get up to tomorrow to further test her chops?

Just then, his bedroom door opened. Carol came into the room wearing nothing but an extra large V-neck T-shirt. The light from the hallway in back of her showed her body in silhouette. "I thought you might still be awake."

"What's up?" he asked. Her long braid hung over her shoulder. She held it with both hands. She looked at the ground. If she was playing the little girl, she was doing a great job.

"I can't sleep by myself. Can I sleep here with you?"

He could see the curve of her body through her shirt, the movement of her breasts as she breathed. She seemed so vulnerable. Was this some sort of game? Was she trying to mind fuck him straight out of the gate? Did she really think she could gain control of him so easily? He shook his head. "Carol, I'm not your boy. We're partners. You sleep in your room."

"But I can't sleep by myself."

"You can't sleep here. Lock your door. Leave the light on. Do whatever you got to do."

He watched her as she sighed, turned, and shut the door behind her. He turned off the table lamp and slid down in the bed. In his mind, he could still see her standing in the doorway. The light falling across her perfect body. He pictured her pulling the T-shirt off over her head and crossing the room toward him. Wait. He looked at the door. Had she expected him to say no? Was she just setting a psychological trap she planned to spring later? He needed to think about something other than her body. Sex with her would be a treat, no doubt, but manipulating men was her default mode. He didn't yet know where he really stood with her, and there was no way she was getting into his bed until he did.

CAROL WENT BACK to her room. She sat on the edge of the bed and hugged herself. Why had she asked Roy if she could sleep with him? Why had she taken that risk? What would she have done if he tried to have sex with her? What was he thinking now? That he could have her whenever he wanted her? She was pretty sure he wouldn't hurt her—that he had her back until they got the job done, that she was safe here and had nothing to worry about on the day-to-day. But all that didn't matter. The night was huge. She felt empty and alone. And she was afraid that if she closed her eyes the nightmares would start. Running in the dark maze. Screaming, being chased, unable to find a way out or a place to hide.

There was only one thing that helped. She needed an anchor. She needed to be lying beside someone who could see her for who she was and wouldn't push her away. But Terry wasn't here. How had his day gone? What had he eaten? Who did he have to fight? Was he thinking of her? She took a slug from the Early Times bottle. The heat from the whiskey felt comforting. She lay down and hugged Terry's pillow and closed her eyes. It was going to be another long night.

5

GRIFTING

The next day at lunchtime Roy and Carol were at the restaurant of the Stillwater Club, a private city club in the downtown business district. They were dressed to blend in: Roy in a sports coat and open-collar shirt, Carol in a sleeveless sundress. They were outside on the terrace at an umbrella table with their dirty dishes in front of them. "Why are we here?" she asked.

"Lunch."

"You're very funny. Why are we *here*?"

"This is a private club, so everyone makes certain assumptions about the type of people they meet here. We can use those assumptions to our advantage."

"How did we get in?"

"I lifted a corporate membership card off a guy a few days ago."

"So what's the game?"

"See those three woman across the way?"

Carol glanced discreetly.

"The one in the middle. Strawberry blonde, short-sleeve dress, lots of jewelry. She just finished her second drink at lunch, and she's been flirting with the waiter, who's probably close to your age. How old do you think she is?"

"I don't know—forty?"

"I'd say about ten years older than me."

"So?"

"When she goes to the bathroom, you're going to follow her. You'll strike up a conversation and come back out at the same time. I'll be waiting. I'll say, 'You ready?' And you'll say to the woman, 'This is my brother, Gary.' I'll shake hands with her. I'll say something like, 'You meet people everywhere you go.' You'll say something. I'll turn to the woman and say something like, 'That's just the way she is. I hope she hasn't been too familiar.' Then we're off to the races."

"What are we doing?"

"I'm going to seduce her. I'm going to gain access to her house and see what I can steal. You'll be waiting in my car."

"You're going to do the seduction?"

"I do it all the time."

"Does this really work?"

"She's day drinking and flirting up the staff. I'm just going to take her where she wants to go."

"What if you get caught?"

"She'll be too embarrassed to call the cops. Can you play your part?"

She nodded.

"What's your name?"

"Leslie."

They paid their bill and slowly sipped their iced teas while they waited for their woman to get up. But instead of her going to the restroom, all three women asked for their checks and settled their bills. Then they all got up together.

"Looks like they're leaving," Carol said.

"Maybe. Follow her just in case."

Carol slid back her chair and started after them. In the lobby, the three women spoke for a moment. Then the strawberry blonde went into the women's restroom while the other two left the club. Carol took a deep breath and followed. In the restroom there were three stalls and a double sink. Carol could hear the woman in a stall. She went to the sink, took out her compact, and pretended to fix her face. A toilet flushed. The woman came out of the stall and went to the other sink to wash her hands. She gave Carol a soft glance.

"There's plenty of room," Carol said.

Carol put away her compact and took out her lipstick, while the woman washed and dried her hands. "That's a pretty color," the woman said.

Carol smiled. "Thanks." She could smell the alcohol on the woman's breath. She held the lipstick out. "Want to try it?"

"Well, I usually wear something more neutral, but why not?"

She used the lipstick and handed it back to Carol. "What's it called?"

"Roseberry Blush. I know. Doesn't make any sense. But it looks good on you."

"Thanks. I'm Penny, by the way."

"Leslie."

They came out of the women's restroom. Roy was waiting. "You ready?" he asked.

"Penny, this is my brother, Gary."

Roy stuck out his hand. "Pleased to meet you."

Penny looked him up and down as she squeezed his hand. "This is your brother? I was going to compliment you on your husband."

They all laughed.

Roy turned to Carol. "Is there any place you don't meet people?"

"Just sharing some lipstick."

He turned to Penny. "I hope she hasn't been too familiar."

Penny put her hand on his arm. Her wedding ring sparkled. "Not at all." She eyed Roy seductively. "Are you in a hurry? Do you want to go for a drink? There's a nice little place just around the corner."

He put his hand on the small of her back as they walked out of the lobby. She didn't pull away.

TWO HOURS LATER, Carol was waiting in Roy's Cadillac on the street in a cul-de-sac in a wealthy neighborhood. She'd excused herself at the bar, picked up the Cadillac, and tailed them here. With Terry, she was the one who did the seduction, so at first this role reversal had seemed like a fun change of pace. But now she was bored and needed to pee. The house she was watching was a two-story Tudor style with a detached garage in the back. The neighborhood was quiet. A UPS truck had just rolled by. It was starting to rain. She wished Roy would hurry up. Just then, a white Mercedes sedan pulled up the driveway. Daddy's home. Carol pictured Roy running out the front door with his pants bundled in his arms. She couldn't help but giggle.

Up in the master bedroom, Roy and Penny were still tangled together in the sheets of the queen-size bed when they heard the back door open and shut. "Penny," a voice called out.

"Shit," Penny said. She scrambled off the bed and pulled her panties on.

"Who is it?"

"My husband. He's early." She hooked her bra and pulled her dress on over her head. Then she stepped into the bathroom.

Roy pulled on his clothes. When Penny came out of the bathroom her hair was back in place. "I'm going to guide him onto the back porch. Go out the front. You can find your own ride, can't you?"

He nodded.

"It's been fun." She gave him a quick kiss and disappeared.

He glanced around the room. He had nothing to fear. The adultery was her problem. He looked through her dresser drawers, found her jewelry, and picked out a pair of diamond earrings. He left the rest. Then he went through her wallet. She had five credit cards. He took two of them. It was time to leave, but there was no reason to get her in trouble if he could avoid it. He made the bed, glanced around to make sure he hadn't dropped anything, and left the bedroom, carrying his shoes in his hands. He walked down the edge of the stairs so that they wouldn't squeak. As he neared the bottom, he could hear Penny and her husband in the kitchen.

"Let's sit on the porch and listen to the rain," she said.

"Let me get out of this suit, first."

Roy crossed to the front hall closet and stepped inside. He heard two sets of footsteps getting closer. "Are you sure you want to change? We're going to dinner later."

"At Tom and Lori's? I don't need a suit for that."

He heard them going up the stairs. He peeked out. They were gone. He wondered what her husband would make of the musky smell in the bedroom. Instead of going out the front, he padded down the hall into the kitchen, slipped on his shoes, and went out the back door. The rain was coming down hard. He ran down the driveway and jumped into the passenger's side of the Cadillac as Carol pulled up in front of the house. He was soaking wet. Carol laughed. "How did it go?"

"You think that was funny?"

"Get a look at yourself."

He shook his head. "Let's get out of here."

The rain continued. Traffic was stop-and-go at major intersections and wherever a school bus stopped to let out children. "So," Carol said, "spill. How much did you get?"

"I got you a pair of diamond earrings."

"Thanks."

"And two credit cards."

"That's all? No cash? I thought there would be more."

"If I took her cash, she'd check through her wallet, find out the cards were missing, and cancel them. This way it could be days before she notices the cards are gone. And when she does figure it out, she's not going to do much. She'll chalk it up to the hazards of casual adultery."

"So what are you going to do with the cards?"

"They're in her name, so I'd have to unload them, but you can use them. You're going to try to buy some very nice ladies' watches. Then you're going to pawn them. We might have time to get started today. So you need to change from younger sister to rich wife."

They stopped back at the apartment. Roy changed into dry slacks and a fresh sports coat. Carol put on a long, floral print dress and Penny's diamond earrings. "You look exactly the part," Roy said.

"Thank you."

The rain had stopped. They drove downtown and parked in front of Fineman's Jewelry and Gifts. It was 4:30 p.m.

"Okay," Roy said. "This is the easy part. You go in. Ask to look at watches. Pick three for around one thousand apiece. Use a card. If it's too much, apologize and use the other card. Remember to sign with Penny's name. If they want an ID, you look through your wallet. Gosh, so embarrassing, you must have left your driver's license at home. Got it?"

"It's that easy?"

"These salespeople work on commission, so they want the sale. You're the trophy wife. Everyone assumes you're innocent. Act innocent. Err on the side of being clueless."

She pushed through the door. She was the only customer. Glass display cases filled with jewelry ran down both sides of the space. The middle-aged saleswoman behind the counter on the right gave her a hopeful look. "Can I help you?"

Carol smiled. "I'm interested in women's watches."

"Any features in particular?"

"Just something very nice." Was the woman noticing her earrings?

"Yes, ma'am." The clerk led her to the women's watches display case.

Carol peered into the case. "Let me look at the Rolex and these other two."

"The Longines and the Omega?"

Carol nodded.

The woman set a velvet board on top of the glass case and placed the watches on the board. "You have a good eye."

"They are all so beautiful." Carol picked them up one at a time to examine them. The prices were in the right range. She looked up at the woman. "I think I deserve all three."

"All three?" The woman smiled.

Carol dug around in her handbag and took out a Visa card in the name of Penelope Davis. The woman read it. "Driver's license?"

Carol made a show of looking through her handbag. "Darn. It must be in my other bag."

Carol watched the sales clerk set the credit card on the glass. She seemed disappointed. How bad did she want this sale?

Carol continued. "Do you really need the ID?" She put on a vulnerable expression and a crumpled smile. "I'm getting some payback on my husband. He's been a snake, and this is how he starts making it up to me." Her eyes watered, and she blinked as if she were about to cry.

The woman looked as if she felt sorry for her. She picked up the credit card and tapped it on the glass. "Okay, just this once. Next time, be sure you have your ID."

Carol blotted her eyes with a tissue. "Thanks so much."

Carol came out of the jewelry store carrying a fancy blue bag. Roy started the car before she got in. "You were right," she said.

"That confidence feels good, doesn't it? Any bumps?"

"She asked for ID, but I hinted that my husband had been cheating on me. I think she completely understood."

"Thinking on your feet. Good job."

"What's next?"

Roy backed out of the parking spot. "It's too close to five to try anywhere else, so we'll have to wait till tomorrow."

LATER, after supper, Carol was leaning back in the passenger's seat watching Roy drive. She'd been with him two days, and she'd learned two new skills—pickpocketing and working stolen credit cards. She'd eaten every meal in a restaurant, she had new clothes, and he hadn't criticized her or raised a hand to her. In every way her life was a step up from what it had been.

"Can I ask you a question?"

"Fire away."

"You get off on the con?"

"Of course. Tell me you don't enjoy the rush of being on the inside of the game."

"How do you decide who to play?"

"It's always easier and safer to work someone who's breaking the rules. You can lead them right where you want them, and they probably won't go to the police. The person who's really honest is a difficult play. Even the jewelry store clerk. She wanted the sale enough to break the rules. My last job with my old partners capsized in part because the mark was too honest. I won't make that mistake again."

"But Penny?"

"Yeah?"

"Why her?"

"How do you feel about mugging drunks?"

"Well, they want to take advantage of me, and most of them are married."

"And Penny is different how? It wasn't a home invasion. She was looking to cheat on her husband. She got screwed over for being a bad player."

"And you fucked her."

"Or she fucked me. I hope I showed her a good time. She never told me to stop or asked me to leave. And, hey, I enjoyed it. Why not?"

"So you'll seduce a woman to set a con in motion?"

He gave her a quick glance. "Where's this going?"

"I don't know. I just never met a guy who—"

"Wasn't the muscle? Or trying to be your pimp?"

"Yeah."

"Glad to broaden your horizons."

Jacob sat in his white Sentra at the freeway rest stop just north of Roosevelt Heights, Ohio. He was parked facing out by the concrete picnic table on the back side of the building. A friend of a friend, a guy he trusted from prison, had told him about a possible job opportunity, one that didn't require a con artist to close the deal, so he'd come here for a meet and greet. The pistol holstered at the small of his back aggravated the pain in his lower spine, but that couldn't be helped. He sipped his coffee and watched the cars pull in, passengers go into the rest stop, come out, and drive off. His contact was late. He was about to give up when a Harley Davidson rolled up and parked next to him. The rider wore a black leather jacket. He took off his helmet. His long hair was in a ponytail, and he had tattoos on the back of his hands. Jacob climbed out of the Sentra.

"You Darius?" he asked.

Darius smiled. "You must be Jacob."

"Who's our mutual friend?" Jacob asked.

"Milt Jackson. Where did you first meet him?"

"Prison transport van. I hear you need partners for a job. Why not use your own people?"

"'Cause the job is ripping off my people. You heard of Jimmy Shane?"

"He's the man in Roosevelt Heights, isn't he?"

Darius nodded. "I want to rip off his weekly take."

"How much?"

"Usually about forty thousand."

"I hear he's an unforgiving bastard."

"You heard right."

"Plan better be tight."

"It is."

"What's my end?"

"I take a quarter; your crew splits the rest. You're responsible for your own overhead."

"And you get paid for?"

"Knowing everything that needs to be known."

"How's that?"

"I'm the one transporting the money."

"So you're staging the robbery?"

"Yep."

"Why do you need us?"

"It has to look legit. So there has to be an actual robbery."

"Okay. I'll collect my guys. You got a phone number I can reach you at?"

Darius gave him a phone number. "You need to call around seven p.m. How long is it going to take to pull your crew together?"

"A couple of days maximum."

CAROL SCURRIED down the hallway in the pitch black. She ran into a door, bounced off it, fell to her knees. Her heart was pounding so hard that she gasped to breathe. She gripped the door handle, jerking it up and down while she banged her shoulder against the door, but it wouldn't open. She could hear shuffling, like footsteps, coming behind her. She fumbled for the light switch on the wall and flipped it up and down. Nothing. She looked over her shoulder, struggling to see in the black. The door. She had to open the door. Something knocked her down. It was on her, touching her, feeling inside her, cold, cold and dead. Its hands were moving up her body to her throat. She screamed.

CAROL'S EYES SNAPPED OPEN. Where was she? Light from the streetlights bled into the room from around the edges of the window blinds. A clock radio sat on the upturned box beside her bed. Roy's apartment. She took a deep breath and ran her hands over her body. She wasn't hurt. She was safe. She wasn't in the nightmare anymore. Her T-shirt was wet with sweat. She looked at the time. 3:00 a.m. She hugged Terry's pillow to her chest. How to stop the nightmares? She closed her eyes and pictured a beach. The tide rolling up the sand, the water advancing and retreating. She tried to breathe along with the waves. Suddenly, the beach was dark. The wind started to howl.

She got up and went down the hall to the bathroom. She used the toilet, rinsed her hands, and drank from the faucet. The apartment was quiet. Was Roy asleep? She went to his room and eased the door open just enough to peek in. She could hear the steady rhythm of his breathing in the dark. What would he do if he found her in his bed? Yell at her? Try to fuck her? He hadn't laid a hand on her thus far. She couldn't go back to her room. She couldn't sit awake waiting for the morning. She padded across to his bed, lifted the covers, and slipped in next to him. He shifted slightly, but he was still asleep. She began to relax. She listened to his breathing, felt his warmth beside her, and closed her eyes.

IN THE MORNING, Roy found Carol in bed beside him. She looked like a little kid, her hair rumpled around her face and a dab of drool at the corner of her mouth. There was definitely something broken in her. She'd snuck in here and hadn't tried to seduce him, the need to lie beside him greater than the fear of what might happen if she did it. Was this brokenness fixable? Was it going to interfere with his plan to get even with his old partners? Or was it just a quirk he'd get used to, like somebody putting ketchup on scrambled eggs? It certainly put their relationship into a strange place, like he was her father or older brother. If he could keep his hands off her, maybe he could work that.

She opened her eyes, saw him watching her, and rolled away from him. "Oh, my God, I thought for a second that it was a dream. But I guess I really did come in here last night."

"I told you that you had to sleep in your own room."

"I can't sleep by myself."

"Are you being straight with me or are you trying to play me?"

She rolled back over to face him. "I'm...I'm being straight with you."

"How long have you been on your own?"

She couldn't meet his gaze. "Since I was fourteen."

"Bad home life?"

"I don't remember much."

"How old are you now? Tell me the truth."

"Seventeen." She gave him a determined look. "I can pull my weight."

"I know it. I don't carry anyone's water, Carol. Just let me ask you this. You afraid someone will hurt you in the night?"

"I don't know. I don't think so. I don't know why I can't sleep by myself. I get nightmares."

"I told you when you partnered with me that I wouldn't hurt you, and that's no bullshit. Do you believe me?"

She nodded.

"You got anything else to say?"

"Can I sleep here tonight?"

"Do you know how crazy that sounds?"

"I know."

"Okay, I can't promise forever, but you can sleep here tonight."

AFTER THEY GOT ready for the day, they got into the Cadillac and pulled out of the apartment complex parking lot. It was a beautiful September morning. The sun was shining, and the grass was green. Children were waiting at the school bus stop in their shorts and T-shirts. On the main thoroughfare, the morning traffic was just beginning to pick up.

"Going to keep working the credit cards?" Carol asked.

"Yeah," Roy replied. "But first we need to go to the Mobil station at the corner of Grand and Lexington. That station has pay-at-the-pump, so we can find out if the card has been cancelled without talking to anyone. That way, worst-case scenario, there's no one to give a description."

They topped off the gas tank at the Mobil station, and then went to breakfast at the Cup-N-Sup. The place was busy with the before-work crowd, but the hostess found them a booth at the windows. The waitress, a sturdy, middle-aged woman dressed in a yellow polyester uniform with a short apron, brought an insulated thermos of coffee and poured coffee for them before she took their orders. Carol ordered scrambled eggs and one piece of toast. Roy ordered the Texas omelet with hash browns.

As soon as the waitress was gone, Roy said, "We'll use the second card here. Then we'll go to a pawnshop, pawn the watches, go to another jewelry store, use the second card, go to another pawnshop, go to another Mobil station with pay-at-the-pump."

"Why not do all the shopping first?"

"If anyone calls the cops, we don't want to be in possession of a lot of jewelry. Three watches is explainable, but nine watches?"

The waitress brought their food. "Anything else right now?"

"Could I borrow your phone book?"

While they ate, Roy looked up the addresses of jewelry stores and pawnshops and wrote them down.

"Why so many?" Carol asked.

"We need upscale jewelry stores and shady pawn shops. We can't walk in just anywhere. We need to increase the likelihood of success."

"And you learned all this how?"

"Partnering with people who knew more than me—people who needed my skills."

"Like your old crew that we're going to rip off."

"Yeah." Roy sipped his coffee. "And I wouldn't be after them if they hadn't screwed me."

The waitress dropped off their check and took the phone book.

"Why did they do it?"

He shrugged. "I was the odd man out. They got greedy and thought they could get away with it. They were right."

He looked at the check and put some money on the table. "Let's go."

"That's a big tip."

"I'm a big tipper."

They paid at the cash register. When they were back in their car and on their way, Carol asked, "Have you ever been in jail?"

"You've got a lot of questions this morning."

"Yeah."

"You ever been in jail?" he asked.

"No," she said.

"I've been inside twice. Stupid little mistakes. Not making them again."

Best Deals Pawns was a storefront located between a vacant lot and Rudy's Tap just north of the downtown. The accordion gate across the front door and windows was open, revealing a display of TVs and radios. Roy pulled into an empty space at the curb. "You know what to do?"

"Yeah."

"Tell me."

"I go up to the counter. I take out the watches one by one, looking at them and hesitating like I don't want to give them up. They should want to give me about a thousand for all three. Too much lower, I walk."

"I'll be just outside, watching through the window. If there's any trouble, I've got your back."

"You sure this will work?"

"It'll work. Just be your usual charming self."

She went into the pawnshop. The window display cases were locked. The shelves were loaded with small appliances and tools. To her right, a heavy-set, dark-haired man with slicked-back hair stood behind a counter enclosed with wire mesh with his hands resting on his beer belly. Jewelry and guns were displayed on the shelves behind him. He grinned. "Can I help you, miss?"

She played her part, reaching slowing into her handbag to take out the watches, trying for a defeated, resigned look. She set them on the counter at the pass-through opening. The pawnbroker watched her hands as she neatened the watches into a row. "I won't be able to give you what you think they're worth."

She sighed. "What's your offer?"

The man folded his arms. "Seven hundred."

She looked up into his face, her eyes pleading. "Is that all?"

He smirked. "You make it worth my while, and I might go up to eight."

"Seven-fifty?"

His voice dropped to a whisper. "Eight hundred with a blowjob."

"I'm leaving." She reached for the watches.

He grabbed her wrist.

"Let go of me," she hissed.

He continued in a low voice. "I bet they're stolen, missy. You cooperate, and I won't call the cops. Only now it's six-fifty for the watches and a blowjob. Best deal you're going to get."

Roy pushed through the door with his .38 in his hand. "Let go of her. Keep your hands above the counter if you don't want to get shot."

The pawnbroker raised his hands. "You can have all the money."

"I don't want all the money. You're the boss here?"

He nodded.

"So it would be a problem for you if this place burned to the ground?"

"Mister, I've got a family to take care of."

Roy glanced at Carol. "What was the deal?"

"Eight hundred if I blew him."

"Eight-fifty it is." He reached into his pocket for his car keys. "Go start the car."

Roy kept his gun trained on the pawnbroker while he counted the money out of the cash drawer. "You call the cops, you get burned down. It's that simple." He scooped up the cash. "Have a nice day."

He backed out of the pawnshop, sprinted across the sidewalk to the Cadillac, and hopped in. Carol pulled out of the parking spot while he was still closing his door. "Hell of a start to the day."

She turned right at the corner. "I could have walked away."

"I wasn't going to give him the watches. Besides, he put his hands on you."

"We could have robbed him."

"Why? So we could get the cops after us? He was a pain in the ass, but as long as he wasn't afraid for his life, he wasn't going to reach for the shotgun under the counter. He'll still make a profit on the watches. His feelings are hurt, but he's going to keep his mouth shut."

She stopped at the red light. "I'm sorry about screwing up."

"How's that?"

"He didn't believe me."

"Of course he didn't believe you. I didn't expect him to."

"Then what was I trying to do?"

"It's about working the percentages, increasing the likelihood that the counter guy will pretend to believe you. That's how shady merchandise moves. You did good. You've got nothing to be sorry for."

6

WORKING THE PLAN

The rest of the day went without incident. They made almost $3,000 before the credit cards were cancelled. Sitting at the kitchen table back at their apartment, Roy counted out the money into two piles. "You did some nice work today."

"Thanks."

"You ready to take the next step?"

"Fill me in."

"One of my ex-partners lives here. You're going to make friends with him and find out where their next job is so that we can be there to steal their score. Can you do that?"

"Do I have to fuck him?"

"Would that be a problem?"

"Well, I—"

"You tell me. If you can't do whatever it takes, we need to know what your limits are now, not when we're in the middle of the con. I pulled a gun in the pawnshop. That wasn't for show. If I had to, I would have shot that guy. No hesitation. Once I pulled the gun, I was committed to going as far as I had to go. If you want success, that's the way it's got to be."

"I can do it."

"You sure? You can back out now. No harm, no foul." He pointed to one of the piles of money. "You'd take eleven hundred dollars with you. That's fifteen hundred minus the three hundred for your clothes and one hundred for overhead. Don't get me wrong. I'd love to have you with me. You're a lot of fun to work with. And if you leave, I've got to find someone new."

"Why do you have to get even with these guys? Why can't we just do some other job?"

"We were partners. They could have just cut me loose. Instead, they set me up, stole from me, tried to get me killed. I'm not letting that go. Are you in?"

"Yes."

"You can do whatever it takes?"

She nodded. "I will."

AFTER DARK they were sitting in the Cadillac among the work trucks and old cars at the far end of the potholed asphalt parking lot of a biker bar located next to a boarded-up factory. Honky-tonk music blasted out of the open windows. A row of motorcycles was parked along the side of the building. A knot of men near the door—long hair, beards, and heavy boots—were smoking marijuana.

"You ready?" Roy asked.

"Do you think I'm dressed right?" She was wearing one of her tiny summer dresses.

"For Pooch? Relax. He's just another mark. He doesn't stand a chance. You sure you can spot him?"

"I've got his picture in my bag."

He squeezed her hand. "Good hunting. And don't worry. I've got your back. Things go sideways, I'll step in."

Carol crossed the parking lot, taking care to avoid the potholes in her high heels. The guys near the door gave her a hard looking over —one of them whistled—but she didn't pay any attention. This was a game she knew, and she was completely at ease. She had her fake ID handy, but the bouncer just nodded. Once inside, she stood for a moment to get her bearings. The waitress moving among the tables was wearing a black leather vest without a shirt under it, tight jeans, and cowgirl boots. The two bearded bartenders were covered in tattoos. The clientele were mainly men and women in jeans and boots, although there were a few women in dresses.

She found a spot at the bar. The man she was looking for was an older guy, bald with a beer belly, probably hanging out with a group of guys just like himself. She ordered a beer. A guy sidled up to her, carefully cut blond hair with an Old Testament beard. He smiled. "How about I pay for that?"

"I'm waiting for someone."

"If you change your mind." He moved down the bar.

She picked up her beer and turned from the bar to look around the room. Back near the pool tables she spotted him. Bald guy, red T-shirt and old jeans, belly hanging over his belt. She checked the picture in her shoulder bag to be sure. Definitely him. What was he doing? He wasn't holding a pool cue. He stepped back to a table where two guys were sitting, picked up a shot glass, and downed its contents. The waitress walked by. It looked like he was flirting her up, and she was ignoring him. She smiled to herself. Getting him out of here shouldn't be too hard.

She took her beer and walked back to the pool table where he was standing. She acted as if she were watching the game. He eyed her, gave a glance around to see if she seemed to be with someone, and then said. "Hey, Sugar, you play?"

"A little bit."

"I bet. I'm up next. You want to be my partner?"

"You going to be mad at me if you lose?"

"I'd never do that."

"I think I'll pass. I'm not really dressed for leaning over a table."

He leered at her. "That is a mighty fine dress. You want a shot of whiskey to go with that beer?"

She smiled. This was going to be way easier than she thought. "You could twist my arm."

. . .

Roy watched Pooch stagger out into the dark parking lot with his arm around Carol. Pooch had more heart than Jacob or Stevie. He wouldn't screw over a partner—at least not on his own—but his ability for self-deception boggled the mind. At this moment, he actually believed that a beautiful young woman would want to have sex with him. Believed it with absolute certainty. Pooch and Carol got into a red Ford pickup truck. Roy started his Cadillac and followed them out of the lot. They drove past the factory and into a neighborhood of small houses with one-car garages. Lights were on behind the drawn curtains, but the streets were dark and quiet. Pooch pulled into the driveway of a tan clapboard ranch. The garage door went up. He drove inside. Roy parked on the street and turned off his headlights.

The light was on in the garage. A workbench and several shelves of tools stood at the back of the space. "Home, sweet home," Pooch said. "Let's get inside, and I'll get you a drink."

He pushed open the door to the kitchen and held the screen door open for her. The kitchen was dark. She stepped inside. He was right behind her. "I hope you're not expecting money."

He pushed her up to the kitchen table. "Hey," she said. "Take it easy."

She tried to turn, but he held her tight with one arm, pulled her panties to one side with his other hand, and took her from behind. She gasped. He was wheezing and banging her against the table with each thrust. She gripped the edge of the table and pushed back to keep her hips from being bruised. She wanted to cry, but instead she thought about beating him with a tire iron and made a couple of fake pleasure noises. In a few minutes he moaned and let go of her. "Sorry, I just couldn't wait. You still want that beer?"

His pants were unzipped. He opened the refrigerator in the dark and handed her a can of beer. He opened his own. "You okay?"

She tried to sound happy. "I'm fine."

He took a drink. "If you need to clean up, the bathroom's just down the hall."

She went into the tiny bathroom, sat down on the toilet in the dark, and pressed the cold can of beer against her forehead. She was going to have to fuck him again. She could smell his breath in her hair and hear his grunting in her ear. Her stomach churned. She swallowed. It was so different when she was in charge, choreographing what was going to happen. Right now she didn't know if he would be gentle or if he was waiting to knock her down and climb on her again. She looked up at the bathroom window. She could climb out and run. Tell Roy she couldn't go through with it. He probably wouldn't hit her. He'd probably still give her the eleven hundred dollars. He seemed like a good guy. But then she would have let that asshole fuck her for nothing. It had to matter. And the only way it would matter was if she got the information. They had to know where the new job was. Talking up marks—that's what she was good at. She needed to get past her emotions and get it done. *You can do this, Carol. Use your magic. Take him into the bedroom and put him on his back. Ride him. Then at least you won't have his weight on you.*

She came out of the bathroom and looked into the dark kitchen. Pooch wasn't there. She walked down the hall to the first bedroom. Empty. She went to the second bedroom. Pooch was sprawled out on the bed, snoring. She stood watching him for a few minutes, just in case he wasn't really asleep, but he was definitely out. How could she find out what she needed to know? She didn't want to be here in the morning. She went over to where his clothes were lying on the floor and went through his pockets. Nothing unusual. She took his wallet, closed the bedroom door, went back to the kitchen, and turned on the light. She took the paper money without counting it and put it in her handbag. There was a credit card, a gas card, and a couple of scraps of paper. Nothing of interest. She left the wallet on the kitchen table and looked around the kitchen. The red light on the answering machine was blinking. She flipped up the lid to read the directions for listening to messages. She pressed play. "You have won —" Next. "Your prescription—" Next. "Pooch. Vacation's over. Meet me in Roosevelt Heights, Ohio, at the Holiday Inn on Sunday at noon."

She turned off the kitchen light and slipped out the front door. Roy flashed his headlights. She ran across the yard and climbed into the Cadillac. "Good news?"

"Yeah. They're meeting in Roosevelt Heights, Ohio." She slumped back in the seat. She should have felt elated, but instead she felt numb.

"You sure?"

"Yeah, I'm sure."

He reached over and patted her arm. "You okay?"

She didn't say anything. She tried to empty her mind, but all she could think about was Pooch grunting and thrusting as he gripped her hips.

Back at the apartment, after Carol had showered and gone to Roy's room, they were lying in bed, the lamp on the night table still on. "So what do we do now?" she asked.

"We go to Roosevelt Heights and shadow them until we figure out what they're up to."

"Won't that be hard to do?"

"If it's just the three of them—if they don't have a grifter—it has to be a smash and grab of some sort. If they've got a new guy, then it gets more complicated. But the hardest part is making sure they don't spot us until it's too late."

She turned away from him. He looked at the back of her head. There was something going on with her—something that wasn't manipulative, something that made her vulnerable. "You've been quiet ever since we got back. What's up?"

"It wasn't what I expected."

"So tell me what happened."

"I don't know if I want to."

"Carol, we're partners. I need to know everything. No judgment, okay? Every little detail might be important to our plan."

She went over what happened, speaking in a neutral voice as if she was talking about someone else's experience.

He sucked on his lip. "So he manhandled you. I'm sorry. I didn't expect that from Pooch. Was that the first time you actually had sex with a man to get him to do what you want? Except for Terry, of course."

She rolled over to face him.

"That is how you keep him wrapped around your finger?"

"That's different. He's my boyfriend. Keeping him happy is just part of the deal."

"And he's always jumped in for the shakedown before you had to do the deed with a mark?"

"Sort of."

"But you kiss the marks, right? You let them feel you up?"

"But I'm in control then."

"Tonight, with Pooch, you were advancing our plan, weren't you?"

"What do you mean?"

"You were using Pooch to advance our plan. It doesn't matter that he thought he was using you. You were in charge. I slept with Penny to steal her credit cards. She thought she was satisfying herself. Did you have a problem with that?"

"No."

"Do you think less of me because I had sex with her?"

"But you're a guy. I give up sex I don't have anything else."

"That's bullshit, Carol. All that matters is that you're advancing our plan."

"So should I have given the pawnshop guy a blowjob?"

"No. We've got a lot of tools in our toolbox. We do what we have to do to manipulate whoever we have to manipulate. Sometimes we talk, sometimes we fuck, sometimes we use a gun. The pawnshop guy was going to cheat you, so it was time to use the gun. The gun wasn't going to work on Pooch." He squeezed her hand. "I'm proud of you. It's hard to do what you did. But you sucked it up, and you put us in play."

He turned off the light. "Get some sleep. Tomorrow we go to Roosevelt Heights."

She nestled in beside him. Then he felt her hand on his chest. "Thank you," she said. She kissed him.

He wondered, for a split second, if this was a mistake, but he didn't push her away. He kissed her back.

THE NEXT MORNING, Carol sat on the edge of the bed in her XL T-shirt looking off across the room. "I was surprised last night."

Roy turned on his side to look at her back. "Why's that?"

She looked over her shoulder. "You slept with me even though I'd just been with Pooch."

"And you slept with me even though you're still with Terry. Or am I missing something?"

"No."

"I told you Pooch was just work. Fuck him, lie to him, hit him with a shovel—it's got nothing to do with who you are."

"But that's not the same as sleeping with you."

"I hope not. I'm not trying to manipulate you, and I hope you're not trying to manipulate me."

She stood up and gave him a sexy smile. "I'm not sorry about sleeping with you—it made me feel better—but I do feel a little guilty about Terry." She twirled her braid. "Just thinking about last night. A lot of guys don't care if a girl gets off."

"You better go get dressed. We've got a lot to do today."

"I thought we were leaving town."

"You know how to shoot?"

"No."

"You need to know how before we start tracking my old partners."

He watched her glide out of the room. For a moment he'd thought she was going to come on to him again. What would he have done then? He believed her when she said she felt guilty about Terry. And yet, here she was flirting with him. It was just natural to her. Where did her feelings end and the manipulation begin? Did she even really know? As it turned out, last night had been exactly the right time to have sex with her. She had needed affirmation that she'd done the right thing letting Pooch screw her, and he'd provided it. She was starting to feel connected to him, and every positive interaction from here on out was only going to reinforce that feeling.

Still, he needed to be careful. He was becoming more certain he could trust her, but he didn't want her to just switch her dependence from Terry to him. He needed her to be independent, capable of making her own decisions; otherwise she wouldn't really be his partner, and he wouldn't be able to count on her in a tough situation. And when she chose him over Terry, it had to be because she thought it was in her own best interest, not because she was afraid she couldn't make it alone.

DURING BREAKFAST AT THE CUP-N-SUP, Roy went through the ads in the *Fredericksburg Gazette*, looking for guns for sale. Only one ad indicated handguns. He called from the phone booth in front of the diner. "Good morning. I'm calling about your ad in the newspaper."

"Yes, sir."

"What handguns have you got?"

"I've only got one handgun left. Colt revolver, forty-four caliber, Sheriff's Special."

"Where are you at?"

"Take Kennedy Boulevard out of town. Take a right on Cypress Hill Road. Two miles out, white farmhouse on the left."

"I'll be there in a few minutes."

"I'll be looking for you."

Roy hung up the phone. Carol was sitting on the hood of the Cadillac, waiting for him. "Well?" she asked.

"This might be our guy. We'll know when we get there."

"How will we know?" she asked.

"We're looking for a criminal or government-hating paranoid. That's the kind of guy we want to buy from—not some law-abiding, gosh shucks suburbanite. Or even worse yet, a retired cop."

They drove out into the country, passing fields of corn and soybeans. The white farmhouse had a picturesque front porch and a picket fence. Two large German shepherds ran toward them barking as they pulled into the gravel drive. A heavyset man who looked like a deranged grandpa, wearing overalls and a seed cap, a shotgun broken down over his left arm, came out on the porch and whistled at the dogs. The dogs ran off behind the house.

"This looks promising," Roy said.

They got out of the Cadillac and walked up onto the porch. "Hey," Roy said, "I just spoke to you on the phone."

The old man eyed them suspiciously. "I figured as much. Come on in."

He led the way into the house. In the living room, a braided rug lay in the center of the floor and an old sofa and chair covered with discount-store bedspreads faced a TV with rabbit ears. The old man motioned on. One of the bedrooms had been turned into an office. An open, roll-top desk sat in the middle of the room and shelves piled with rifles and accessories ran around the walls. On the desk sat the Colt Sheriff's Special.

"There you go."

Roy picked up the pistol, released the cylinder, looked down the barrel from both ends, snapped the cylinder back into place, and spun it. "What do you want for it?"

The old man snapped the shotgun closed and pointed it down. "What do you think it's worth?"

"The serial numbers have been filed off."

The old man shrugged. "Mighty handy if you need to drop it."

"Can't explain it to the cops."

"Then don't let them find it."

"I'll give you five hundred for it."

The old man shook his head.

"Six hundred if you kick in a box of shells."

The old man reached around on the shelf behind him and then put a box of shells down next to the gun. "You can load it when you're off my property."

Roy laid six one-hundred-dollar bills down on the desk. The old man picked up the top one and held it up to the light. He nodded.

"Is there a place around here where a man could pop off a few rounds without drawing attention?"

"Turn left out of here, turn right at the second crossroad. You'll come to an old quarry a few miles down."

"Thanks."

"You've never been here."

"You're exactly right."

The quarry was a long limestone scar in the wasteland beside a farm field planted in corn. Roy drove down the dirt road and parked out of sight of the highway under a scraggly tree. The ground was littered with cigarette butts, fast-food trash, and condoms. Steel drums and crates of various sizes had been set up at different distances to make a shooting range. "This is definitely the place," Roy said. "But I don't want you starting with the .44. Too much kick. We'll use my .38."

Roy put the .44 and its shells in the trunk of the Cadillac and brought out his Smith & Wesson .38. "Come on."

They walked over to the shooting range. "First off," he said, showing her the gun, "this is a tool. You don't take it out unless you need to use it. You don't point it at anyone you don't plan on shooting. You don't hold it with your finger on the trigger. You always assume it's loaded."

He pointed at a crate about fifteen feet away. "Let's shoot at that one. That's as far as you'll ever need to shoot right now. Watch me." He held the gun in a two-handed grip. "I'm using both hands so that I've got the most control. I'm going to point at the crate, take a firm grip, aim down the barrel so the front and back sights line up, and squeeze the trigger. Just squeeze it."

He stood with his right leg slightly back and his left leg forward, raised his arms, and shot off a round into the center of the crate. "Nothing to it." He handed the gun to her.

She mimicked what he had done and hit the left center of the crate. "Wow. This is easier than I thought."

"Fire a few more. Use a little more of your trigger finger."

She shot twice more with the same results. She grinned. "This is fun."

He nodded. "The gun range is always lots of fun. But when you're scared and someone's shooting back, it's a little different. So you've got to know what you're doing."

They heard a car coming down the road. "Hand me the gun."

Roy put the .38 in his jacket pocket just as a sheriff's department cruiser came into view. They stood with their hands at their sides while the cruiser stopped, and a uniformed sheriff's deputy got out. "Hello, folks. I heard some shots as I was driving by."

Roy spoke. "We were just firing off a few rounds, sir."

The deputy had his hand resting on the butt of his holstered pistol. His eyes shifted from Roy to Carol and back. "You're carrying?

"Yes, sir."

"You have a carry permit?"

"Yes, sir."

"How about you, ma'am?"

"I don't have a gun."

The deputy stepped forward. "Where's your gun, sir?"

"In my jacket pocket."

The deputy gripped the butt of his pistol. "I want you to hand me that gun. Move one hand only."

"I'm moving my right hand." Roy slowly reached into his pocket and took out the .38, holding it out in the palm of his hand. The deputy took it. "Any other guns?"

"No, sir."

The deputy released the cylinder on the .38 and shook the remaining bullets and spent shells out into the palm of his hand. Then he handed Roy the empty gun and the shells. Roy put them back in his jacket pocket.

"Let me see that permit."

"In my back pocket." Roy took the permit out of his wallet.

The deputy glanced at it. "Mr. Stevens, this is private property.

We've had some trouble here in the past. The owners don't want people trespassing."

"I'm sorry, sir. We must have been given some bad advice. We were just looking for a place to practice."

Carol cut in. "It's all my fault, Deputy. I've been begging my cousin to teach me to shoot. I hope I didn't get him into trouble."

The deputy glanced at her. She gave him the soft, appreciative look that always worked on the marks. He turned back to Roy. "There's a gun range in town. I don't want to see you out here again." He handed Roy's permit back to him. "Get moving."

"Yes, sir."

Roy and Carol got in the Cadillac and drove back out to the road. "That was a close call. Thanks for pitching in. If he had searched the trunk and found the Colt, we would have been on our way to jail."

"Then what?"

"We would have had to post bail and skip town. Change our names. Guns would have been lost. Just a lot of hassles that would have messed up our timeline."

"You wouldn't have left me?"

"Leave you? Have I been showing you what I know? Helping you to make your own way?"

"Yes."

"Why would I invest the time if I was going to dump you? You're going to be watching my back. Jacob, Stevie, and Pooch are going to wish they never even thought about screwing me over when I get through with them. And don't you want some payback of your own on Pooch?"

"So are we going to the gun range in town?"

"No, that's way too public for us. It's time we got going anyway. It'll take most of the day to drive to Roosevelt Heights."

"I have to see Terry first."

A DEPUTY SHERIFF ushered Carol into the visitor's room of the county jail. The room contained a row of cubicles that faced a matching set of cubicles on the other side of a glass partition. The walls were yellow. Women were sitting in most of the cubicles, leaning on the tiny desks as they talked on the phones with their men on the other side of the glass, whispering for privacy. Terry was already there. He was dressed in orange coveralls. He had a mark under his left eye, and there were scabs on the knuckles on his right hand. She sat down in the cubicle facing him. She kissed her hand and pressed it against the glass. He picked up his phone. She picked up hers.

"Hey," he said.

"How are you holding up?"

"I'm finding my way."

"You've been fighting."

He shrugged. "What are you doing for money? I could use some cash in my commissary account."

"How much? A hundred?"

"Where would you get a hundred bucks?"

"I'm working with Roy—the Cadillac guy. He's teaching me some new tricks."

Terry frowned. "I told you to stay away from him."

"This is different. I can't work our game by myself. This is the only way I can make any money."

"I don't trust that guy."

"Don't worry. I've got everything under control."

He studied her face. "You're already sleeping with him."

"I am not."

"Don't lie to me."

"I'm not lying. I'm doing everything I can for us. You just need to stay strong."

"Bullshit. You're fucking him."

"Don't be jealous. You're my guy. I'm just working with him until you get out."

"You're going to do what I say."

"Don't be like that."

"Stay away from that guy."

"Really, Terry, how can I make a living—"

He slammed the phone down and scooted away from the table. She watched him mouth the words "do what I say," and he was gone. She stood up. God, why did he always have to be such a jealous pain in the ass? If the glass hadn't been between them, he would have smacked her for sure. It was a good thing she lied about the sex. That would have made him even crazier. He'd be picking fights with other prisoners over nothing if he really believed she'd slept with Roy. But she'd made the right decision partnering with him. Everything she was learning was going to come in handy when Terry got out of jail. Once he saw that, he'd feel differently about what she'd done.

On her way out, she stopped at the clerk's window in the outer waiting area and deposited $100 into Terry's commissary account. Visitors—women and children mainly—sat in plastic chairs waiting their turns. There wasn't a happy face in the room. She was glad when she finally pushed through the door to the parking lot. Roy was waiting for her in the Cadillac.

"How did it go?" he asked.

"I told him I was working with you."

"How did he take it?"

"How do you think?"

"If Terry was a player and not just muscle, you wouldn't have been rolling drunks and he wouldn't have ended up in jail. You'd have been picking pockets, and he'd have been using the credit cards. Safe and easy."

"Yeah."

"You're doing the right thing. This is your best shot to helping Terry and helping yourself."

"I know." She looked out the window. "He accused me of having sex with you."

"I see."

"I told him I didn't. And I'm not going to anymore."

"That's your call."

7

SHADOWING THE MARKS

Sunday at 12:30 p.m., Roy and Carol were sitting in their Cadillac on the street two houses down from the little house on Elm Street where Jacob, Stevie, and Pooch had parked. They'd followed them from the Roosevelt Heights Holiday Inn. The neighborhood consisted of shabby rentals occasionally interspersed with well-maintained residences where old people sat on the porches.

"So this is where they're at?" Carol asked.

"Jacob likes this kind of setup. It's easy to blend in. You keep your nose clean, you keep quiet, nobody notices you."

"Where are we going to stay?"

"Someplace even more nondescript."

They drove out to the freeway interchange and turned onto the access road. Roy ignored the value motels with their tourists and business travelers. Finally, on the corner of a side road, he spotted a rundown rent-by-the-week motel. Half the lights in the street sign didn't work. A number of old cars were parked in the far side of the lot.

"Really?" Carol asked. "This place is a dump."

"The trailer park I found you in? Look who's talking."

They got a room at the end of a row. The beds were worn out, the towels were thin, and the tub had rust stains. Carol set her suitcase down on the bed closest to the door. "I'd pull off that bedspread," Roy said.

Carol looked at him quizzically.

"I doubt if the hookers around here are so choosy about getting in the sheets."

She made a face.

"No one's going to find us here. That's what counts."

"Which bed are we going to sleep in?"

"If you're sleeping in the same bed as me, that's the one farthest from the door." He set his suitcase in the floor of the closet. "And I wouldn't unpack. We might have to leave in a hurry."

"So what's next?"

"We're going to drive around—learn this town, cut down on the number of possible surprises. Tomorrow we start tailing the guys."

LATER THAT AFTERNOON, Jacob, Stevie, Pooch, and Darius were standing in the kitchen of the Elm Street house. Darius hadn't bothered to take off his motorcycle jacket. They all had beers in their hands. A city map was spread out on the kitchen table. "Listen up," Darius said. He pointed with a tattooed hand. "The black dots are cars Jimmy has parked on the street to hold drugs or cash for delivery. These two circles are houses he uses. One is a collection point. The other—his girlfriend's—is where the money finally lands."

"And these locations never change?" Jacob asked.

"The cars move around, but I know where they are all the time."

"So how we going to do this?" Stevie asked.

"Hit the girlfriend's house?" Pooch asked.

Darius shook his head. "Ellie's house is the wild card. The money always ends up there, but I don't know how long it stays there. Jimmy doesn't trust anyone that much. I carry the money from the collection house."

"The Jackson Street house?" Stevie asked.

"Yeah. So you guys are going to hijack me along the way." He pointed at the map. "There's a shuttered Save-U-Mart right here. It's on the most direct route, but there's very little traffic, so chances are nobody's in the way."

"You're alone?" Jacob asked.

"Always. Driving a minivan."

"So we divide the money at the Save-U-Mart and go our separate ways."

Darius shook his head. "It has to look real. You guys are going to T-bone me, come out running and gunning. That way there's a wrecked van and bullet holes."

"So when do we do it?"

"Friday. We take in the weekly cash from the street dealers on Friday, so that's the big day."

"Why are you even doing this?" Jacob asked. "You could just be skimming."

"Three guys count the money. How long do you think three guys can keep a secret?" Darius looked from Jacob to Stevie to Pooch. "We done here?"

Jacob nodded. "Here's the phone number for this place. Keep us posted."

Darius left. Stevie was looking at the map, studying the streets. Pooch got another beer. "So all we have to do is gear up and wait until Friday."

"No," Jacob said. "We're going to check out the stash cars and stash houses. We want to know who all the players are. We don't want any surprises when we pull this job, and we're going to be sure Darius isn't fucking with us."

Shortly after 8:00 a.m. the next morning, Roy and Carol drove through a Caffeination coffee shop for coffee and two egg croissants on their way to the Elm Street rental. The traffic was bumper-to-bumper on Richardson Drive, but once they were on the other side of the business district, it was clear sailing. Elm Street was just as quiet as it had been the day before.

Carol scrunched up her croissant wrapper and put it in her empty coffee cup. "You know we're way conspicuous on this street, don't you?"

"We'll be okay today. Then we'll decide what we need to do."

A little before 10:00 a.m., Stevie pulled out of the driveway in a blue Dodge Charger. "Here we go," Roy said. "We drew the short straw. He's their driver, so if he spots us, he'll probably shake us."

They followed Stevie down into the southeast part of town into a neighborhood of mainly blacks and Latinos. He pulled into the on-street parking next to a row of well-kept ranch houses with wrought iron fences. They drove past him, came around the block, and parked half a block back on the other side of the street.

"Why's he here?" Carol asked.

"Don't know, but I want to see him and whatever he might be looking at. Can you see the street sign?"

"Sycamore."

About an hour later, a white man wearing a hoody and jeans and carrying a book bag over his shoulder opened the trunk of a tan Toyota Corolla up near the end of the block, put his bag in, took out an identical bag, and walked away. Stevie pulled away from the curb. Roy followed him.

"What was that?" Carol asked.

"Not really sure. We'll have to see."

They followed Stevie into another neighborhood, this one middle-class and white, and parked on Jackson Street next to a strip of brick, two-story homes. A mom came out of one of the houses pushing a baby stroller. A twenty-something man wandered down the sidewalk walking three dogs. The mom and the young man chatted for a moment before continuing in opposite directions. After a while the mom circled back home. The occasional car drove by. Finally, about two hours later, the white man who'd been wearing the hoody earlier pulled into a driveway in a white Subaru and got out carrying four book bags. He went into the house. A few minutes later, he came out empty-handed and drove away. Stevie followed him, and they followed Stevie. The man left the Subaru parked at the North-gate shopping mall and went to the bus stop. They followed Stevie back to Elm Street.

"So what's happening?" Carol asked.

"Hoody guy must be gathering drugs or drug money from around town. That would be my guess. Stevie was shadowing him, which means they're probably planning to rob this crew. We need more pieces of the puzzle."

BACK ON JACKSON STREET, in a house with a real estate agent's *For Sale* sign in the yard, a state investigator and a city detective working on a drug taskforce sat on kitchen chairs at the living room windows watching the money collection house through the curtains. A video camera on a tripod stood in front of them. Clark Benson, the state investigator, a thin ex-smoker in a leather jacket and jeans, turned off the camera. "That was definitely Bobby Reese making the delivery."

"Yeah," Tom Smiley, the city detective, said. He was a pudgy guy with a gray mustache who was dressed in a blue blazer and tan slacks. "But what was up with the other mopes? The redheaded guy in the blue Dodge watching the house, and the couple in the Caddie watching him. I've never seen them before."

"Maybe Jimmy's gone paranoid. Maybe he's got someone following Bobby to make sure he isn't dipping," Benson said.

"But what about the other two?"

"Who knows? We need to take all their pictures if they show up again. See if they're in the database."

"If they're in the game, maybe we'll be able to scoop them up as well."

"Always the optimist."

THE NEXT MORNING, Roy and Carol followed Pooch as he left the Elm Street house in his red Ford pickup truck. He parked in the metered parking on Twelfth Street near a corner convenience store. They circled around to find a spot behind him. When they were parked, they saw him come out of the corner store with a six-pack of beer. They sat there for over an hour before a tall black man who wore his hair in cornrows stopped at a silver Taurus, opened the trunk, took out a black book bag, and then got in the driver's seat and drove away. Pooch followed him, and they followed Pooch.

The Taurus drove into a blighted neighborhood and pulled to a stop in front of a boarded-up building. A black kid, maybe fourteen, wearing basketball clothes, came out of a doorway, got in the car for a minute, and got out carrying a paper sack. The Taurus made two more stops in rundown neighborhoods and then drove out to the eastern suburbs. It pulled to the curb half a block from a high school. A green Lexus pulled up. A white high school kid wearing expensive casual clothes jumped out, jogged over to the Taurus, slid in without shutting the door, and jogged back to the Lexus with a bulge under his shirt. Then the Taurus drove back into town and found a parking spot on Twelfth Street, one block north of the corner store.

"Uh-oh," Roy said. "Look at the gray work van."

Carol looked up the block on the other side of the street. "Is that a camera?"

"Taking pictures of the Taurus. Must be the cops."

Pooch slowed down in front of them and made a U-turn in the intersection. "Jesus," Roy said. He held up his hand to block his face, and Carol ducked down in her seat. Pooch drove right by them.

"Do you think he saw us?" she asked.

They drove past the work van. Roy took a left at the corner. "Don't know. Right now I'm more worried about the cops. We've seen them, so we've got to assume they've seen us."

He took the next right. "Keep a look-out for anyone following us."

She turned in the seat.

He took another left into a residential neighborhood, sped up to the next stop sign, took a right, and circled the block.

"There's no one behind us," she said.

"You sure?"

"Yeah."

"Okay. The cops are set up on that Taurus. They might also be on the Sycamore car or the Jackson Street house. Worst-case scenario, they've taken our pictures three times already."

"What are we going to do?"

"Change cars and move."

They drove down to Orion Avenue where a number of car dealerships were located and pulled into Dollar Bill's Used Cars. After an hour of haggling, they left in a white Ford Bronco with rusted fenders. They drove through a Taco Grande for some late lunch on their way back to the motel, where they cleared out their room, wiped it down, and left.

"Can we go to a better motel this time?" Carol asked.

"I don't think there are any worse," Roy said.

They got on the beltway and got off at another interchange where billboards advertised motels. "How about the Econo Inn?" Roy asked.

"Why that one?"

"Straight shot onto the freeway."

They got a room on the first floor on the side closest to the parking lot exit. The room was bright, the bedspreads were clean, and the bathroom fixtures were reasonably new. Carol left her suitcase on the floor by the door. "So we're still trying to rip off your old partners."

"Yeah."

"What about the cops?"

"Carol, we don't want the cops taking our pictures, but we're just spectators here. All we're doing is driving around town. We aren't breaking any laws. If my old partners rob that drug crew and escape with the cash, we rip them off. If their plan goes wrong, and they get killed or arrested, we stay out of the way. There's no downside for us."

"Then why did we change motels?"

"Because, if my old partners rob the drug crew, and it gets messy, we don't want the cops dragging us in for questioning right when we need to be chasing the money."

· · ·

"HEY, GUYS." Pooch sat down on the sofa in the living room of the Elm Street house. A game show was on the TV. Jacob was sitting in a La-Z-Boy recliner, and Stevie was coming back from the kitchen with a can of beer in his hand.

"Where you been?" Jacob asked.

"Did you guys see any cops today?"

"Not me," Jacob said.

"Cops were set up on Twelfth Street watching the Taurus. I think I got away without being seen."

"You think?"

"Definitely wasn't followed. I've been circling around for a couple of hours. And I saw Paul. He was in a light blue Caddie with this little girl I fucked last week."

"Which explains how he got here." Jacob drummed his fingers on his thigh. "He must have been following you."

"I didn't tell the girl anything."

"We should have shot him," Stevie said.

"The kid's luckier than Jesus. Cicilie Chandler's friends should have killed him," Jacob said.

"So what now?" Pooch asked.

"We've got to figure out if the cops are watching the Jackson Street house. We don't want to be seen until it's too late."

"What about Paul?" Stevie asked.

"He doesn't want to get in the middle of this. That's not his style. He was following Pooch, so he's probably hoping to rip us off, which means we've got nothing to worry about until we have the money. Then if he shows up, we kill him."

JIMMY SHANE GOT out of his Chevy Blazer in a downtown parking ramp close by O'Brian's Barbeque. He was a big man with a shaved head. He was wearing a blue suit with a white shirt and no tie, but he moved like a brawler looking for a fight. The sidewalks were busy with the after-work crowd leaving from happy hour or going to dinner. He glanced at his watch. He was late. His girlfriend, Ellie, would already be sitting at their table, tapping her foot and watching the door, but he needed to make a phone call before he got to the restaurant. He spotted a phone booth in front of a Gas and Go Convenience Mart and crossed the street. He dialed city detective Tom Smiley. "Hey, Smiley."

"Jimmy, what's up?"

"Somebody in a red Ford truck was tailing my delivery guy."

"Really? It isn't one of us. You know where our guys are."

"You don't have anything new going on?"

"Nada. You know everything we know."

"I want you to look into this."

"No problem. Who was being followed?"

"The Twelfth Street Taurus."

"I'll get it sorted out."

"ASAP."

"Of course."

Jimmy hung up the phone. The money he paid Smiley was money well spent. The drug taskforce never collected enough evidence to do anything but arrest a few of his lowest level street dealers. And the cops were always good for squeezing the competition. O'Brian's Barbeque was just up ahead. Jimmy grinned. He was looking forward to a big plate of ribs.

LATER THAT EVENING, Smiley met Benson at the Jackson Street *For Sale* house. They stood in the dark in the living room by the kitchen chairs positioned near the windows and peeked through the curtains at the money collection house across the street. The lights were on in the downstairs, and a minivan was parked in the driveway. "It's been quiet since seven o'clock," Benson said.

They walked back into the kitchen and turned on the lights. Photos and reports were stacked on the kitchen counter. "Anything new today?" Smiley asked.

"The Twelfth Street surveillance team spotted two cars following Jimmy's guy. Just like the mopes we saw yesterday on Jackson Street, only the guy in the first car was different. It looks more and more like somebody's planning to rip off Jimmy."

"How much longer until we have enough evidence?"

"We're close. We just need video of Jimmy handling the money. We've got all the other pieces of the puzzle. But we can't wait too long. If some idiots try to rob him, it'll turn into a mess," Benson said.

"As long as it's players killing players."

"It's never players killing players. Jerkoffs never hit what they're shooting at."

Smiley shrugged. "Did we track either of the cars?"

"Kelly and Sue managed to follow one car to a motel. Man and a woman. Watched them check out, change cars, and move to another motel. It's in the report. They must have spotted the van. The other car, we don't know where it went."

"That's a tough break. We need to get all these players under surveillance if we're going to stay ahead of any trouble."

DARIUS STOOD in the living room of his doublewide trailer with an unopened fifth of Jim Beam in his hand. His woman, Melody, was in the kitchen getting a glass out of the cabinets. She was a skinny little bleached blonde whose pregnant belly stuck straight out in front of her, straining the fabric of her untucked shirt. She brought him the glass. He hugged her and kissed her neck. Then he sat down on the sofa, opened the bottle, and poured while Melody got a Coke from the refrigerator.

"How's my little man?" he asked.

She smiled. "He was kicking hard after lunch."

"You been getting everything ready?"

"Yeah."

"But not working too hard?"

"I'm taking it easy." She sat down beside him and put her swollen feet up on the coffee table.

"Nobody knows we're leaving?"

"I haven't told anyone."

"Not even Katie?"

"Especially not her."

"We're set for Friday. Then we're gone."

"You still think your sister will be glad to see us?"

"When she sees we're starting a family, that I'm looking for a job, that we've got money to tide us over, she'll be fine."

"We could go to my mom's."

"All your friends know where your mom lives. Jimmy would be on us in days."

"Are you really, really sure about this?"

"I'm not getting busted again and going back to prison. I've got you and the little man to take care of. Besides, I'm setting up these jokers I'm working with to take the fall. Jimmy will blame them. Everything is going to be fine for us."

"I hope so." She cuddled up against him.

He put his arm around her. "Trust me, Mel. We're going to make a fresh start."

LATE WEDNESDAY MORNING, Roy and Carol were tailing Jacob, who was driving a white Nissan Sentra. He left the Elm Street house, stopped for gas at the People's Mini-Mart, made a phone call from the pay phone, and then parked on the street with a view of the Jackson Street house. Over the course of the next four hours, three guys showed up to drop off book bags, no one staying in the house for longer than twenty minutes. Finally, just before five o'clock, the black man with the cornrows came out of the house with a large gym bag and got into the minivan. Jacob didn't follow him. Instead, he drove into an older neighborhood of small Cape Cod houses just south of downtown and parked on the street next to a neighborhood park with monkey bars and teeter-totters and a *No Dog Walking* sign. Roy and Carol parked half a block back. Thirty minutes later, the minivan pulled into the driveway of a house across from the park. The black man got out with the gym bag, went inside for about fifteen minutes, came out without the bag, and drove away. Jacob left in the opposite direction. But Roy didn't follow him; he just kept looking at the house.

"What's up?" Carol asked.

Roy rubbed his chin. "How do they know where these houses and parked cars are located? Stevie and Pooch got here when we did, right?"

She nodded.

"Maybe Jacob has been here a couple of months, figuring it all out. Hunt and peck. Or maybe they have a partner feeding them inside information. That's the most likely."

"How does that affect us?"

"Someone else to look out for—someone we don't know."

"So they're going to rob this house?"

"No, I don't think so. I think they're going to try to pull the money from the cars or ambush the delivery guy before he gets here. That's why they've been checking up on the cars and houses and following those guys around town. If they were going to rob the house, why would they risk being noticed?"

"But what about the cops?" she asked.

"We know they're set up on the Twelfth Street car. We know about the Jackson Street house, so I bet they do, too. Hell, they may know about all the drops, cars, and houses. But that doesn't matter to us. We're not robbing the drug crew or interfering with the cops. That's the beauty of our plan. No dealer and no cops. And if there's an inside man, our plan makes even better sense. We just need to make sure we're tailing Jacob and the guys when they pull the job, so that we'll be able to rip them off when they drop their guard."

THAT EVENING, Jacob, Stevie, and Pooch were sitting in the living room of the Elm Street rental, eating delivery pizza from the box and drinking beer. Baseball was playing on the TV. Jacob muted the sound. "So now we've seen it all—the stash cars, the three guys who do the pick-ups and drop-offs, the collection house, and the girlfriend's house where the money ends up. Looks like Darius is playing it straight with us."

Pooch reached for another piece of pizza. "We gonna keep his cut?"

"We could, but that's just extra aggravation. Right now everything is safe and easy. On Friday Darius comes out of the Jackson Street house with the gym bag, and we make it look like it's a straight-up robbery."

"Boom," Stevie said.

"Exactly," Jacob said. "No muss, no fuss. The Charger is the fastest, so we move the Sentra and the truck ahead of time, and use the Charger for the getaway car. We're already packed, we get the money, and we leave town like a bat out of hell."

"That's two more days," Pooch said.

"Two days to find out where Paul is staying and put a first strike on him."

"Now you're talking," Stevie said.

"Thought we were going to let him come to us," Pooch said.

"We've got the time. Might as well use it. How was that girl he's got with him? Is she worth a try?"

Roy woke with a start. Carol was yelling incoherently and thrashing about beside him. He turned on his bedside lamp. "Carol." He shook her shoulder. "Carol."

She sprang up, looking around the room, her T-shirt hanging from her thin frame.

"You were dreaming. Hollering."

She put her hand on her chest. "That was crazy."

"You need a drink of water?" He got up, filled a plastic cup from the bathroom sink, and brought it to her.

She took the cup from him. "That was the weirdest, realest dream I ever had."

"What happened?"

"I was in some kind of time loop. It was me and Terry. We were doing our thing, but every time something went wrong—I got raped or stabbed or Terry got shot or arrested—and then it all started over again. Nothing I could do could make things turn out right." She gulped the water.

He took the empty cup from her. "He'll be out in a few months."

"I know."

"It wasn't your fault. You know that, right? You were working his game—stealing cars, rolling drunks. It's only a matter of time before it all goes wrong. The odds were against you."

"I know that now."

"He made his choice. He should have known the risks. I don't claim to have all the answers, but you're not going to end up in a trap like that with me. We're going to steal from people who won't go to the police. And if you don't like my plan, if I won't listen to your suggestions, you can walk away. No hard feelings. By the time we're done dealing with my old partners, you'll have learned everything you need to know to make your own way."

She slid back down in the bed. "Why are you so good to me?"

"Carol, in this life you have to have some rules you live by. We're partners. It's us against the world. You need a drink of that whiskey you've got hidden around here?"

"No, I'm okay. I'll be okay."

He turned off the light. She snuggled up against him. Everything was going according to plan. He'd won her trust, even if she still felt loyal to Terry. He was the one on the scene, the one she was lying next to, the one she was looking to for comfort. Soon she would be his woman, and she'd choose him over Terry. Soon it would be time to tell her the truth about how Terry ended up in jail.

The next afternoon, they were following the black man with the cornrows as he drove around town making deliveries. They knew his route so they kept well back. When he reached the Jackson Street house, they parked at the far corner just in case there was police surveillance they didn't know about. When the minivan pulled out, they followed. The minivan drove a circuitous route, doubling back on itself twice, but it eventually ended up at the Cape Cod. No ambush. No carjacking.

They drove over to the Elm Street house. The truck and the Sentra were parked in the driveway. "I guess nothing's happening today," Roy said.

"Maybe they're going to rob the Cape Cod."

"The minivan is the easy score."

They were driving back to their motel, cutting through a residential neighborhood, when an unmarked police car, an Impala, turned on its lights and siren. They pulled over in front of a duplex. A fat man with a gray mustache, wearing a blazer and slacks, a pistol holstered on his hip, got out of the Impala. Roy lowered his window. The fat man showed him a city detective's badge.

"What's up, sir?" Roy asked.

"Registration and license."

"Temporary registration and bill of sale are in the glove box, and my license is in my wallet."

The detective nodded. Roy got his wallet out of his back pocket and produced his driver's license. Carol passed him the temporary car registration and bill of sale. He handed both to the detective. The detective examined them both and handed them back.

"Mr. Stevens, you've been interfering in police business."

Roy looked at him quizzically. "I'm not sure—"

The detective shook his head. "You keep acting stupid, you're going to make me angry."

"We don't want any trouble."

"Then quit following those guys you've been following. Do you understand?"

"Yes, sir."

"I better not see you again."

Roy watched the detective in his side mirror until he got back into the Impala and drove off.

"So we're all done," Carol said.

"No. It's only going to be a few more days. I can feel it. We just need to be more careful, and we need a new car."

"We're going to trade in the Bronco?"

"No. Any legit car is just going to lead to me. I'll steal something for tomorrow."

Roy drove around in circles for a while, just in case anyone else was following them. They ate dinner at The Pasta House, a chain spaghetti restaurant near their motel. Then they stopped at a Quick Shop to fill up their gas tank and buy some snacks before they went back to their room.

The parking spaces in front of their room were full, so they parked across the lot. Carol got out of the car carrying a bag of snacks and a six-pack of beer. "Where will you get a car tomorrow?"

Roy locked the car. "Find a long-term parking lot. Train station is a good bet. We'll only need the car for a few hours."

Roy led the way. Just as he came to the door to their room, room key in hand, Stevie sprang out of the shadows and sucker-punched him in the side of the head. Roy staggered off balance. Stevie stepped forward and punched him in the gut. Roy folded up. Carol gasped. The snacks and the six-pack fell out of her arms. Roy scrambled around a breezeway post. Carol scurried backward across the parking lot, looking for other attackers. Roy caught Stevie on the chin with a right cross and shifted back behind the post, but Stevie charged after him. Carol spun around. *The Bronco.* She shoved her hand into her handbag, searching for the spare car keys, but her hand found the butt of the Smith & Wesson. She pulled it out, glanced at Stevie and Roy struggling on the breezeway, looked at the gun. She couldn't do it, could she? Stevie grabbed Roy by the throat and started banging his head against the wall. Christ. She had to help him. She raised the .38. She was too far away. Without thinking, she rushed up behind Stevie, shoved the pistol into his back, and pulled the trigger. The gun clicked.

Stevie's head swiveled. Roy tore free of Stevie's grip, pushed past him, and snatched the gun from Carol's hand. Then he pivoted and backhanded the pistol hard into Stevie's face. Blood sprayed onto his clothes. Stevie staggered. Roy hit him again, the barrel of the gun striking Stevie's temple. He fell to the pavement, his face a bloody mess. Roy kicked him. Stevie didn't move. Roy glanced around the parking lot. No one was watching. He leaned against a nearby car to catch his breath. "Thanks."

"I didn't think I could do it," she said.

"But you did. You saved my ass. I'm not going to forget it."

"I wanted to run."

"Everybody wants to run."

"Why didn't the gun go off?"

"It was on an empty chamber. If you'd pulled the trigger again, you would have woken up the neighborhood." He spotted the Dodge Charger parked two cars down. "Hell, there's his car. Help me drag him to it."

"Is he dead?"

"No. I should kill him. He deserves it. But that might spook the other two. We're going to take their score before I deal them out. Give me a hand. We need to get out of here."

They dragged Stevie to his car and loaded him into the back seat. "Pooch must have seen us. We should have been paying more attention, should have been looking for their cars. We need to move every day from here on out."

They got their suitcases from the motel room, picked up the six-pack and the snacks from the pavement on their way to the Bronco, and drove onto the beltway. "Where to?"

"The next interchange should be fine."

"The cops have warned us off."

"Yeah."

"Your old partners know we're here."

"What's your point?"

"Is it too dangerous?"

"I won't lie to you. The clock is ticking. We can't be around here much longer, that's for sure. But I still think we can rip them off. Will you trust me on it?"

"Okay." She nodded. "I'll trust you."

· · ·

DARIUS AND BOBBY REESE were sitting in a gray Volvo in the parking lot of the Light Fantastic Gentlemen's Club. It was Jimmy Shane's money laundry. There'd been fights there the last few nights, and Jimmy had sent them there in case the bouncers needed extra help.

Bobby patted the pistol in the pocket of his hoody. "Your old lady will be pissed if she finds out you were here."

Darius shifted in his seat. "She knows it's just business."

"Woman that pregnant ain't thinking straight. She's thinking about how long it's been since you been fucked."

"How the hell would you know?"

"I'm just saying—"

"You're just saying bullshit. That woman be on me night and day if I was home."

"Man, that's not a picture I want in my head."

"Then shut the fuck up."

They sat for a while watching men go into the club. Finally, Darius said, "Hey, you notice those cars fluttering around the edges of our pick-ups and deliveries?"

"Yeah. I told Jimmy. He took care of that," Bobby said.

"How's that?"

"He put Smiley on it."

"I don't trust Smiley."

"Why not?"

"Because he's a cop. He'd sell us out to save himself every time."

"Jimmy trusts him."

"Jimmy pays him; he don't trust him."

"So what do you want to do?"

"Tomorrow's the big money day. If somebody wanted to jack us, that's their best day to try. Tony's doing collections. You're supposed to be off. You hang back, stay out of sight at Jackson Street. When I leave out of there with the money, you follow me. If those guys ambush me, you follow them, tell the boss where they are."

"Let them take the cash?"

"Jimmy will want them all dead. We get in a gunfight, maybe we win—maybe we don't. If you follow them, find out where they're at, Jimmy can send a crew to clean them up."

"What about you?"

"Dead or alive, you won't be able to help me."

"Okay, I'll be waiting to follow you."

"Great," Darius said. "Of course, nothing's going to happen."

Bobby smiled. "You're right. Nothing's going to happen."

STEVIE STAGGERED into the Elm Street house, his eyes black and the front of his shirt bloody. Pooch jumped up from the sofa. "Jesus Christ! What happened to you?"

"Fucking Paul broke my nose."

Jacob came out of a bedroom. "You were supposed to phone us."

They followed Stevie into the kitchen. He went to the sink, splashed cool water on his face, and patted his face dry with paper towels.

"All swelled up, but not so bad with the blood off," Pooch said. "A touch crooked to the right, though."

"Straighten it out," Stevie said.

Pooch put his hands on both sides of Stevie's nose and applied gentle pressure.

"Jesus fuck, how about taking it easy?" Stevie said.

"You want it straight?" Pooch said. He lowered his hands. "That looks better."

Jacob got a beer from the refrigerator and handed it to Stevie, who held the can against the side of his nose.

"Where was he?" Jacob asked.

"Econo Inn out at the end of Greene Boulevard."

"How did the kid take you?" Pooch asked. "He's not much of a fighter."

"I had him until the girl put a gun on me. Lucky I didn't get shot."

Pooch chuckled. "That little girl pulled a gun?"

"Fuck you."

"Well, he's gone now," Jacob said.

"I know it."

"Maybe he's been scared off," Pooch said.

"Are you kidding? He's not going to give up for nothing. Would you?" Jacob asked.

Pooch shrugged.

"We're just going to have to keep our eyes open. Good thing this job is already in the bag."

"I want him," Stevie said. "I want to fuck him up and then kill him. And that girl's going to take a beating."

"You need to settle down, hoss," Pooch said, "or that nose will start bleeding again."

"We got to get them," Stevie said.

"Don't worry," Jacob said. "He's going to turn up. He has to. He can't leave well enough alone. When he tries for the money, we'll take him and the girl."

Roy AND CAROL were in a room on the backside of the Budget 8 Inn, the last motel on the access road at the next interchange. Roy was sitting up in bed with a plastic bag of ice pressed against his face. The local news was on the TV, but there was no report of an altercation at the Econo Inn or of a man found in a car.

"How are you feeling?" Carol asked.

"Fine, really, other than the bruised face."

"So we're still on our plan?"

"Steal a car, set up on the Jackson Street house, don't let the cops see us, follow the minivan. If the guys strike, follow them, take the money."

"What if they're ready for us?"

"Of course they plan to be ready for us. But we get to choose our time. They can't be on their guard every minute. They're going to believe they've outrun us, they're going to party, and we're going to get the money."

"But what if they catch us in the act?"

"If we're past the point of no return, then we'll have to shoot it out."

"Roy, I don't know—"

"I know you don't know. You're still afraid you might run. That's okay. Everyone starts out that way. Don't worry about it."

"Did you?"

"Oh, yeah, first time out, I was scared half to death and afraid my partners would find out."

"Your ice is melted."

She took the bag of ice into the bathroom where she'd put the ice bucket. She looked at herself in the mirror. She didn't know why—why at this moment—but she wanted to have sex with him, wanted to feel the physical intimacy that matched the emotional intimacy she felt. She didn't care what she'd told Terry. She still felt loyal to him. It was like an old habit she couldn't give up, but she knew now she didn't love him anymore. What she felt for Roy—it was something new and deep that she couldn't yet put into words. He'd said that she'd saved his ass. She smiled to herself. She'd done that. She'd made that choice. She felt so, felt so—what? Free wasn't the right word. She wanted him inside her.

When she came out of the bathroom carrying the ice bag, she was naked. Her long dark braid hung over one shoulder and swayed with her breasts as she sashayed across the room to the bed. She watched Roy watching her. She knew she was going to get her way. She handed him the ice bag. "You see something you like?"

He set the ice bag on his night table without taking his eyes off her. "God, you really are beautiful."

She climbed onto him and started unbuttoning his bloody shirt.

"Why are you doing this?"

"Because I want to."

"You think it's a good idea?"

"Don't care." She leaned down and kissed his lips.

. . .

LATER IN THE NIGHT, Roy lay beside her, watching her sleep—her relaxed, open expression, her soft breathing, the occasional flutter of her eyelids. The first time they had sex, after Pooch jumped her, she'd needed affirmation that having sex with marks didn't taint her, and he'd given her that. But this time, she'd made love to him, given herself emotionally as well as physically, simply as a gift. They were completely intimate now. Their relationship was exactly where he wanted it to be. So if they were going to continue together, there couldn't be a lie between them. They had to be skin on skin. As soon as this job was over, he was going to tell her the truth about how Terry got arrested. And then she would have to decide if she would stay with him or go back to Fredericksburg to wait for her boy.

8

THE ROBBERY

Friday afternoon, Roy and Carol were sitting in a stolen Chevy Monte Carlo a block back from the Jackson Street house on the other side of the street. Roy was wearing a ball cap, wraparound sunglasses, and a black windbreaker. Carol was wearing a blonde wig and a gray raincoat. It was raining, fat drops coming down hard, so there were no pedestrians on the sidewalks or children playing outdoors. Half a block up, on the same side of the street as the money collection house, the Dodge Charger sat at the curb. Since Roy and Carol had started watching, three different men had made deliveries to the Jackson Street house. It was almost 5:00 p.m. when a ponytailed man in a leather jacket came out of the house with a gym bag, jogged over to the minivan, and drove away. The Charger started after the minivan, and Roy and Carol followed the Charger.

Thunder boomed. The windshield wipers could barely keep up with the downpour, but Roy managed to keep the Charger and the minivan in view. As the minivan approached the parking lot of a shut-tered Save-U-Mart discount store, a white Suburban sped through a stop sign and rammed into its front end, crashing it into a light post. The Charger pulled over. Roy and Carol slid to a stop about half a block back. Two men wearing face masks and carrying assault rifles jumped out of the Suburban and rushed through the torrent to the wrecked minivan.

"Looks like Stevie and Pooch," Roy said.

IN THE MINIVAN, Darius spat out his mouth guard. The airbags were deflating. He had the gym bag in his lap and a sawed-off shotgun across his knees. When Stevie jerked open the van door, Darius pointed the shotgun.

"Relax, bro," Pooch said. "It's all good."

Darius unzipped the bag. There were five bundles of money. Four of them were labeled "$10,000." He took one of the $10,000 bundles and slipped it into his jacket. "Just as agreed."

Stevie nodded. Pooch grabbed the gym bag.

"Hold up," Darius said. "This needs to sound real." He pulled a pistol from his pocket, fired it into the roof, and then fired the shotgun into the back of the van.

ROY AND CAROL heard the gunfire and watched as the two men disappeared with the gym bag into the Save-U-Mart parking lot. "Damn rain," Carol said. "Can't see anything."

"The guy in the Charger isn't being left behind."

When the Charger pulled back into traffic, they followed. It turned left at the stoplight, turned right at the next corner, and right again six blocks later. A Ford Explorer was sitting in the parking lot of the All-Trust Independent Insurance Agency. The Charger pulled up beside it, and Pooch and Stevie climbed out with the gym bag and the rifles and got in. The Charger drove three blocks down to Greene Boulevard, turned left, and headed for the freeway interchange, Roy and Carol following two cars behind.

. . .

Darius got out of the wrecked minivan and jogged through the rain to the black pickup truck that he'd parked on the street. He sat down in the truck and smoothed his wet hair back out of his face. His end of the take—$10,000—was tucked inside his jacket. He'd seen Bobby drive by, following Stevie and Pooch, so there was only one thing left for him to do. He drove to the Shell station on the corner of First Street and used the pay phone.

"Jimmy?"

"Yeah?"

"We've been jacked."

"What?"

"Some guys T-boned me and took the bag."

"Where?"

"At the old Save-U-Mart."

"Son of a bitch."

"Bobby is tailing them."

"How's that?"

"We were talking the other night, thought there might be trouble since those cars have been following the pick-ups, so I had him following me."

"You okay?"

"Yeah."

"What was the take?"

"Forty-three thousand, six hundred and forty."

"Get back here."

"On my way."

Darius hung up and called home. "Melody?"

"Yeah, baby."

"I'll be there in a few minutes. Be ready to go." He got back into the pickup truck. The dominos were falling just right. Jimmy and the guys were going to be completely focused on Jacob and his crew until they killed them and got the money back. By the time Jimmy found out the money was short, he and Mel would be way down the road. He'd secured a new life for his family. He smiled to himself. Jimmy was never going to see him again.

. . .

BOBBY CUT across the Save-U-Mart parking lot in an old Ford Pinto and watched the two hijackers climb into a black Ford Explorer. Darius had been right. Smiley was worthless. He hoped Darius was okay, but he couldn't stop to check. He had to keep after the Explorer. If he lost the money, there would be hell to pay. The rain started to let up. He was parked on the street across from All-Trust Independent Insurance Agency when a blue Dodge Charger pulled up, and the two guys with the gym bag got out of the Explorer and climbed into it. But something was strange. It seemed as if a red Monte Carlo was also following the money. There it was, just ahead of him as he followed the Charger down Greene Boulevard. He glanced at the shotgun on the seat beside him. That was Jimmy's money. If the people in the Monte Carlo got in the way, he was going to deal with them.

THREE HOURS LATER, Bobby followed the blue Dodge Charger and the Monte Carlo into the Econo Inn parking lot at the freeway interchange outside Indian Grove. The Charger parked between a red Ford truck and a white Sentra and the Monte Carlo drove to the end of the lot and parked facing the motel. Three guys got out of the Charger and went into room 107 on the ground floor. Bobby made a U-turn and drove to the Mobil station on the access road to use the pay phone. "Jimmy? It's Bobby."

"Where are you?"

"I'm in Indian Grove. The hijackers are in the Econo Inn at the freeway. Room 107."

"Good work. You stick with them. We're on the way."

SMILEY CAME in the back door of the surveillance house and walked through to the living room, where two detectives assigned to the drug taskforce, a man and a woman, were watching the Jackson Street house. He peeked through the curtain. Two cars were in the driveway and another was at the curb.

"It's been crazy busy over there since about five-fifteen," the woman said.

"Like this?" Smiley asked.

"We've counted three different cars and six players," the man said.

Smiley went into the kitchen and called Benson at home. "Clark? Sorry to bother you. Jimmy is rounding up his people. Something's up."

"Today's collection day, isn't it? Do you see any of the mopes who were following Jimmy's guys?"

"I warned off the one crew. You think the other one actually knocked over Jimmy's van?"

"See what you can find out."

JIMMY SHANE SAT at a folding table in the back storeroom of the Light Fantastic Gentlemen's Club talking with two lieutenants: Juan, a squat Latino with a tiny goatee, and Bruce, a tall black man who wore his hair in cornrows. The bass beat of some stripper's favorite song pounded through the closed door from the main stage. "Bobby called. We know where the hijackers are."

"How you want to handle this?" Bruce asked.

"We're going to kill these assholes so dead that no one will ever try this again." He turned to Juan. "Did you break out the heavy gear?"

"Already in the cars," Juan said.

"And both your crews are ready to go?"

They nodded.

"Either of you seen Darius?"

They shook their heads.

"Anybody call Melody?"

"I had Shirley call," Bruce said, "but nobody answered the phone."

"Send Pat to check on her."

. . .

Roy and Carol sat in the Monte Carlo watching the door to the motel room. The rain stopped just after nightfall, but the heavy cloud cover hid the moon and the stars. A silver Lincoln Town Car pulled up. Three black women, their breasts and asses bulging out of dresses that could only be called gift wrap, got out, knocked on the door to 107, and went inside.

"Working girls," Roy said. "They're settling in."

"So how do we get the money?" Carol asked.

"They usually leave the loot in one of the cars so that their company can't steal it."

"So that would be the Charger. What are we waiting for?"

"Want to make sure they've got everything they need. Did they order delivery food? More liquor? Drugs?"

Carol sat back in her seat. "I don't like waiting."

"We need something to eat. Go get us some coffee and sandwiches. I'll keep watch." He climbed out of the driver's seat. Carol slid over. He walked along the parked cars until he reached the breezeway, his hands in the pockets of his jacket. The .44 Sheriff's Special was holstered at his hip. Thus far, everything was going according to plan. A little patience and they would have the money and be long gone before the guys knew it was missing. They might even blame the hookers. He kept his eyes on the door.

A few minutes later, a China Delight delivery car pulled up, and a teenager got out with two large sacks. Roy stepped back around the corner of the building. There was a dumpster behind him and an open field. When he looked back down the breezeway the delivery car was gone.

Carol came back and parked where they were before. Roy climbed in the passenger's side. "Anything?" Carol asked.

"Chinese delivery. What did you get?"

"Tuna and an egg salad. Which do you want?"

"I'll take the tuna."

She passed him a sandwich wrapped in waxed paper and a large cup of coffee. "Thanks," he said.

While they were eating, Pooch came out, barefoot and shirt unbuttoned, went into his truck for a moment, and then went back into the motel room. "They're a restless bunch," Roy said.

"The girls have been in there over an hour," Carol said.

"They usually don't keep them all night."

They sipped their coffee and waited. Finally, Roy said, "I'm going to take a leak around the back of the building. Then I'm going to have a look in the Charger's trunk. Why don't you get the .38 out of your handbag?"

He went back around the side of the building to the dumpster, peed, and then walked nonchalantly down the breezeway toward the Charger. The curtains were tightly closed on the room. He peered into the Charger. It was empty except for the usual fast-food trash. He went around the back and used one of his shanked car keys to open the trunk. Nothing. Just as he was shutting the trunk lid, the motel room door opened. Roy crouched, grabbed the bumper, and slid under the car. He could hear the prostitutes talking as they came through the door. The door closed. He saw their high-heeled shoes as they walked by the Charger.

He slid out the side between the Charger and the Sentra and crouched between the cars, counted to ten, and then peeked at the front of the motel room. Everything was quiet. The guys had gone straight into the motel room when they arrived. They hadn't stopped anywhere. The money had to be with them. Still, Roy had to check. He looked through the Sentra's windows. Nothing. He popped the trunk. There was a suitcase of clothes and a canvas bag that contained lock picks, shanked keys, a slim jim, and other burglary tools. He took the bag. The truck cab was empty. He walked down the breezeway and along the parked cars until he was back at the Monte Carlo. He tossed the burglary tools into the back seat and got in the front.

"What you got?" Carol asked.

"Just burglary tools."

"So the money is in there with them?"

"Seems so."

"So we're screwed."

"If they divide the money up before they leave here, yeah. Then we'd have to track them individually. But if they go somewhere else first, we could still be in business."

"What do we do now?"

"Wait."

"I'm taking a nap." She got into the back seat and lay down. Roy slid in behind the wheel.

BOBBY SAT in his old Ford Pinto at the other end of the parking lot, sipping a Pepsi and watching the motel room door. What was up with that couple in the Monte Carlo? Why did the guy search those vehicles? Did he know about the money, or was he just breaking into promising cars? Bobby put his hand on the butt of his shotgun. If they got in the way, he could deal with those two on his own. He could probably get the money back on his own, for that matter. There were only three of them. They were drunk and overconfident by now. He had the element of surprise. But Jimmy had said to wait. So that was what he was going to do, unless everything suddenly went crazy.

THE INTERIOR DOOR between rooms 107 and 108 was open. In room 108, both beds had been used, and damp towels lay strewn on the carpet. In room 107, the bed closest to the bathroom had been used, and open Chinese delivery boxes, beer cans, and an empty whiskey bottle littered the table and the dresser top. Jacob and Stevie sat in their underwear at the table, beers in front of them, while Pooch sat on the unused bed.

"How many of those girls did you screw?" Stevie asked.

"I fucked the tall one and Charese," Jacob said. "That was plenty for me."

"Charese the dark one?" Stevie asked.

"Yeah."

"She was good."

"You got that right."

"I screwed all three of them," Pooch said.

"You're lying," Stevie said. "You were just laying there. They were fucking you."

They all laughed.

"Easy money," Pooch said.

"None easier," Jacob replied.

"I wish the kid had showed," Stevie said. "I would have loved to mess him up."

"He still could," Jacob said. "He knows how we work. He could have followed us. That's why the money's not in the car."

Pooch patted the mattress he was sitting on.

"Either the kid shows up, and we kill him and the girl, or we leave here tomorrow, and we never see him again. Either way works for me," Jacob said.

Stevie snorted. "I still want him dead."

THE GETAWAY

A Ford Explorer followed by a Subaru wagon swung into the Econo Inn parking lot, moving fast. The Explorer flashed its lights at Bobby's Pinto as it flew by. The cars screeched to a stop in front of the motel room. Eight men wearing Kevlar vests and armed with shotguns and assault rifles jumped out of the cars, ran up to the room, and blasted through the doors and windows. Bobby ran across the parking lot to join in.

"Just in time, bro," Bruce said.

Jimmy kicked in the broken door. The men swarmed into the room, firing as they came.

"All clear," someone yelled.

"All clear," came the reply.

All three of the hijackers were dead, lying in their own blood, shot multiple times before they could even grab their weapons.

"Where's the money?" Jimmy yelled.

They searched through the rooms, checked the dressers and the bathrooms, and upended the mattresses. "Found it," Juan said. He pulled the gym bag from a cavity inside the box spring of the unused bed.

Jimmy poked around in the gym bag. "It's about ten thousand light."

They broke into the three cars parked in front of the room. Nothing. Bobby looked for the Monte Carlo. It was gone.

JUST AS JIMMY'S crew squealed to a stop in front of the motel room, Roy started the Monte Carlo, but he didn't turn on the headlights. "Carol. Seat belt."

Carol climbed back into the front seat. She saw the Kevlared men rush out of their cars and open fire. Light flashed from the muzzles of the guns in the dark like a scene from a war movie. The noise was deafening. "Jesus."

"Hold on." Roy pushed the Monte Carlo into reverse, bumped over the curb, and backed across the grass until he was clear of the other parked cars. Then he spun ninety degrees, pushed the car into Drive, and stomped on the gas. The car tore across the lawn to the access road and bounced down the curb. Roy turned on the headlights and sped for the freeway interchange. He looked in the rearview mirror. There was no one behind them.

"Those guys must be dead," Carol said.

"They were assholes. What did you think we were going to do to them after we stole their score?"

"I didn't think about it."

Roy made a right turn onto the freeway ramp. "You don't really care what happened to them, do you?"

"No, I just don't want to end up dead." She glanced back toward the motel one last time. "Where are we going?"

"Back to Roosevelt Heights. We need to pick up our stuff and get out of town."

"So we're all done?"

"Yeah. Nothing left here but pain and suffering. I know I promised you more, but that's the way it goes."

· · ·

TOM SMILEY STOOD in the phone booth at the Chevron station across the divided highway from the Econo Inn. People were out of their cars, watching the gunfight. "Yeah, Clark, Indian Grove. Need the local swat team if they've got one. Jimmy's crew is shooting up the Econo Inn. Hold on."

He took the phone away from his ear. He could hear sirens: one, two, three cars.

"Cops are almost here. What do you want me to do?"

"What a mess," Benson said. "There's no reason for anyone to know you're there. Come on back. We'll make contact with the local police tomorrow, offer to share information. If Jimmy doesn't get arrested, maybe we can still get video of him handling the drug money."

"See you in a few hours."

Smiley got into his car. He had plenty of gas. He drove back toward the freeway. A patrol car, lights flashing and siren screaming, sped by on the other side of the divided highway. Smiley shook his head. Jimmy was radioactive now. There was no way he could help him anymore. Not with a murder rap hanging over him. Those mopes who'd robbed him had sure screwed up. But what about the couple he'd warned off. Were they still hanging around Roosevelt Heights? Did they know what was going on and would they try to take advantage? He might be able to make a few dollars there.

TWO POLICE CRUISERS, lights flashing, screeched to a stop in the Econo Inn parking lot just beyond the Explorer and the Subaru. Jimmy and his crew ran back into the rooms just as the officers got out with their shotguns.

"Grab the mattresses," Bruce said.

Jimmy's men dragged the mattresses up against the bullet-riddled front wall and hunkered down behind them. Jimmy went back into the bathroom, Juan and two other guys following in his wake. There was a window in the wall above the toilet.

"Break it out," Jimmy said.

Juan stood on the toilet and broke out the glass with the butt of his rifle. There was an open field behind the motel. "All clear, boss."

Jimmy set down his rifle and took off his Kevlar vest. "Everybody scatter. We'll meet back at the club."

He climbed out the window with the gym bag over his shoulder and started jogging down to the end of the building. He could hear the police loudspeaker, but he couldn't make out what it was saying.

ROY AND CAROL drove in silence for a while. Fog rose from the wet fields along the freeway, making it difficult to see in the distance. After they passed a road sign indicating Roosevelt Heights was thirty miles away, Roy glanced at Carol. "What's your plan?"

"What do you mean?"

"You want me to drop you back in Fredericksburg or are you going to stay with me? I'm guessing we've still got about eight hundred dollars apiece."

"I promised Terry I'd help him."

"You sure you going back to him?"

She studied his face in the dim from the dashboard. "I don't know."

"You think you can train him to change up his game?"

"No. That's what has me worried. Next time it could be me going to jail."

"I want you to stay with me. You're smart. You've got the magic. But I've got no use for Terry. And Terry's got no use for me."

"I know."

"I've got feelings for you, and I think you have feelings for me. So I want you to make a good decision. A decision you won't regret. Do you know how Terry got busted?"

"Bad luck. The mark fought back."

"No. I called the cops."

"What? You called the cops?"

"Yes."

"You motherfucker!"

"I wanted to see what you could do, and I wanted you to see what you could do. But Terry wouldn't cooperate, so I had to take him out of the picture."

"How can you expect me to trust you?"

"Because I'm telling you the truth—even though I don't have to."

"You're a bastard."

"Maybe, but I don't lie to a partner."

She looked out her window into the dark. He'd ratted out Terry, got him busted, made him suffer. Even if she didn't love him anymore, that was wrong. And Roy had manipulated her into becoming his partner. He'd been sitting in that diner with his story all ready. But from the moment she'd agreed to help him, he'd always done everything that he said he would. And now she had the skills to take care of herself. Or was that just his game? His way of manipulating her to get her to choose him over Terry. Terry was a puppy dog. Her puppy dog. But he had sharp teeth. She could get him to do anything, as long as he thought it was his idea, and as long as he thought he was in control of her. If she went back to him, it would just be more of the same. She glanced at Roy. Terry'd be angry right now if she'd yelled at him like she'd just yelled at Roy. He'd pull over, yell at her—maybe slap her. But Roy? He never raised his voice or hit her. Why had he really told her about what he did to Terry? Had he just assumed that she would eventually find out or had he been telling the truth? That there couldn't be a lie between them?

They didn't speak anymore on the way back to Roosevelt Heights. Roy took the exit ramp onto Greene Boulevard and the access road to the Budget 8 Inn. The parking lot was half empty, and there was no one hanging about. Roy pulled into the spot in front of their room. "So what's it going to be?"

"I don't know. I'm still mad at you."

They went into the room to get their suitcases. Carol looked at the bed they'd made love in the night before. Even though she was still angry, she knew she was going to forgive him—had to forgive him. She felt completely safe with him. Knew that he wanted her to be just who she was, that with him she wouldn't have to pretend. She sighed.

The last few days started cascading through her mind—the parked cars, following the guys, the Jackson Street house, and the Cape Cod. She turned to Roy.

"There were a bunch of guys at the Econo Inn in Indian Grove, weren't there?"

"Yeah?"

"So how many guys are in that drug crew?"

"You mean how many are here in town right now?"

"Yeah. We know there's probably no money at Jackson Street, but is there any money at the Cape Cod?"

Roy nodded. "I like the way you think. But if it's guarded, there's no way."

"But what if it's not? What if they're all in Indian Grove? If there's a safe, can you crack it?"

"It depends. I've been learning from Jacob, but I'm no expert."

"But you took Jacob's tools."

"That's not the same thing as experience."

"So we should skip it?"

"I didn't say that. I'm saying don't get your hopes up."

They drove south through the city. The Friday night traffic was busy near the Civic Auditorium. Just south of downtown, they took a right turn onto Ninth Street. Up ahead on the right was the neighborhood park, and across the street was the small Cape Cod. Roy pulled up to the curb at the park. The night was still overcast. The house was dark. There were no cars parked in the driveway.

"Looks innocent enough," Carol said.

"Let's do it."

Roy got the bag of burglary tools out of the back seat and dug around in the bag until he found two flashlights. They walked quickly across the street and up the driveway to the back of the house. The backyard was quiet. No dogs barked. Roy turned on his flashlight. The doorknob was ancient, but a new deadbolt had been installed above it.

"Well?" Carol asked.

"No problem. Keep your light on the lock." He picked the lock and eased the door open. They were standing in the kitchen. The stairs to the basement were to their left. They moved through the living room and up the stairs to the bedrooms, their flashlights showing the way. Two of the bedrooms were empty. The largest one contained a king-size bed and a dresser. Women's clothes hung in the closet, and shoes littered the floor. There was no money in the dresser drawers, there were no shoeboxes full of cash in the closet, and there was no safe.

They went back downstairs. They looked in the TV cabinet and under the sofa and chairs, just in case, but they found nothing. They went back into the kitchen and shined their lights on the door to the basement stairs. It was steel.

Roy studied the deadbolt. "This one's going to be harder."

He worked at it for a few minutes with the lock picks. Finally, the bolt slid back. He pulled the door open. It was pitch black. "Windows must be sealed," Carol said.

Roy found the light switch and flipped it on. They went down the wooden stairs. The basement was concrete block. Plywood was nailed over the windows. Against the far wall, a small safe was bolted to the floor. Next to it, a money counting machine sat on a folding table.

"I don't know, Carol. This might be beyond me."

"We're already here."

"You're right. Go upstairs and watch out the window."

She disappeared up the stairs.

Roy looked over the surfaces of the safe, the money-counting machine, and the folding table, just in case someone had written down the combination. It seemed counterintuitive—stupid, really—but people often left the combination jotted down on the wall or on a piece of tape stuck to the bottom of a nearby surface. Never underestimate a mark's laziness—that was one of Jacob's sayings. No such luck tonight. Roy opened the burglary tool bag and pulled out a laminated card that contained a list of "try out" combinations that manufacturers supplied with new safes. He tried the four that matched this brand of safe, but Jimmy must have reset the combination. He took a deep breath. He needed to relax. There was nothing to lose and everything to gain. Jacob had shown him how to crack a safe old-school, but he hadn't ever done one by himself.

He squatted in front of the safe and spun the dial to get a fresh start. The "try out" combination list indicated that this safe had a three-number combination, which meant three notched wheels that had to be lined up for the safe to open. He turned the dial slowly, listening for the clicks that indicated the edges of each notch in each of the wheels. He graphed the results until he had the numbers—sixteen, fifty-seven, nine—and wrote out the six possible combinations. Then he tried them all. The door wouldn't open. One of the numbers must have been wrong.

He started over, but he got the same result. He rechecked the safe brand against the "try out" combination list. It was definitely a three-number combination. He stood up and ran his hands through his hair. The money was right here. There had to be a way to get to it. He scanned the room again. Nothing here except the folding table and the money counter. He lay down on his back and used his flashlight to look at the bottom of the folding table, but the result was no different from when he'd glanced under it to begin with. He picked up the money counter and looked at the bottom. No tape. No scratchy writing. Just a model number. 16AFG23H09.

Wait a minute. Two of the numbers were the same as the likely combination numbers. Maybe he was going to finally catch a break. He tried the model numbers—sixteen, twenty-three, nine—in various orders. On the fifth try, the door opened. He smiled to himself. Jimmy was one sneaky bastard—just not sneaky enough.

Inside the safe was a plastic bag of money and a Colt .45 automatic. Roy shut the safe and started up the stairs. Carol met him in the kitchen.

"I got lucky," he said.

She smiled in the gloom. "How much?"

He opened the bag on the kitchen table. There were two bundles wrapped with rubber bands, each marked $10,000. He handed one bundle to her. She chuckled. He put the other bundle in his jacket pocket and picked up the bag of burglary tools. "Let's get out of here."

They turned off the basement lights and locked the doors on their way out. The neighborhood was quiet as they scurried down the driveway and across the street to the Monte Carlo.

Just as Roy was opening the driver's door, a man got out of the car parked behind them and started toward them. It was the fat city detective who'd stopped them yesterday. His hand was resting on the gun holstered at his hip.

"You two are the nerviest mopes I've seen in a long time."

"What are you talking about?" Roy asked.

"How much was in the safe?"

"What?"

"Don't play dumb. I'm guessing breaking and entering, possession of an illegal firearm and burglary tools, and that's before I run your prints. I'm a reasonable guy. Give me the money and get out of here."

Roy thought about the .44 he was carrying. Was this cop really dirty? He didn't want to shoot him if he didn't have to, but he wasn't going to jail. He set the bag of burglary tools on the pavement. "I'm reaching for the money." He took the rubber-banded bundle out of his jacket pocket. "How about if we split it fifty-fifty?"

The detective shook his head. "That's my money."

"Not even a finder's fee?"

"Walking away is your finder's fee."

Roy handed him the bundle of bills. The detective riffled through it with his thumb before he slipped it into his sports coat pocket. "Is this all there was?"

"Yeah."

He peered at Carol. "How about you, young lady? You carrying any money?"

"No," she said. There was a tremor in her voice.

"How old are you?"

"Old enough."

He sniggered. "Already a tough guy, huh? How about if I pat you down?"

She turned and put her hands on the fender of the Monte Carlo.

Roy watched the detective look from him to Carol and back. Roy shifted his hand to get closer to the .44. What was the detective thinking? If he made two steps, he was going in the trunk alive or dead.

But the detective didn't step forward. He just snorted and turned to Roy. "Hand me that bag."

Roy handed him the bag of burglary tools. The detective opened it. The .45 from the safe was sitting on top. "Well, well."

"Can I at least have the bag back?"

"No. Get out of here before I change my mind."

Roy and Carol got into the Monte Carlo. The detective was still standing in the street holding the bag of burglary tools when they made a right turn at the first stop sign. "That cop knew way too much," Carol said.

"But you played it well. We still have half the money, and we didn't have to kill him."

"Where are we going?"

"To the train station. We're going to put this car back into the long-term parking and pick up the Bronco."

They drove north through town. The streets were quiet except for the occasional pedestrian or dog walker. Neither one spoke for a while.

Finally, Roy said, "Well, that's five thousand apiece, plus the eight hundred. Not as much as I hoped, but a lot more than you've ever seen at one time. After we switch cars, what do you want me to do? You still haven't told me."

She watched him drive. He was asking her what she wanted. Did he already know the answer or was he really waiting to find out? Was that how his game worked? He gained her trust by actually caring about her and catering to her needs? If so, it was the subtlest form of manipulation she'd ever seen. She shook her head. Roy had definitely worked his magic on her. Looking back now, she could see how it had happened—all the care he'd taken to win her over. He'd been wooing her from the very beginning. She wondered if she could learn to charm him as well as he'd charmed her. He would make a real challenge, not like Terry or the marks they'd hunted. "What are you going to do?"

"Find a score big enough so that I can go on a long vacation."

"How long?"

"Two or three months."

"Won't be much fun by yourself."

"Probably not."

"Maybe I should come along."

He smiled. "That sounds like a great idea."

He stopped in the left turn lane at a traffic light. "I know a guy that may have a lead on a job. Couldn't much use him before. Need a man and a woman team for a lot of jobs."

"I can leave whenever I want?"

"You're a free woman." He turned onto Jensen Boulevard. The train station was up ahead on the right.

"I'm not saying that I'm your girl."

"I know."

"So we really are partners?"

"Yeah."

"You know my real name. What's yours?"

"Paul Kendal. But I won't be using it, and you won't be using Carol. We're going to change names and get new IDs. It just makes everything easier."

"So where are we going next?"

"We're going to get out of this town, spend the night at a motel on the interstate. Tomorrow I'll call my guy and see what kind of job we can get lined up."

"You think we can really do this?"

He flashed a smile. "Honey, us, together, we're going to have a really good time."

-The End-

A Note from the Author

So that's how the Travelers met and first teamed up over twenty-five years ago.

She's learned the tricks she needs to know to be on her way to becoming a master grifter. And he's found the partner he needs to take his game to the next level.

But now we're off to the present, where their relationship and their skills will be tested to the limit in a series of can't-figure-them-out thrillers.

Will you join me?

Read about scheming partners, get more insider crime craft, and hold onto your seats as vengeful enemies come looking for payback in the *The Traveling Man: The Travelers Book One*.

Turn the page for a sample from chapter one.

A SAMPLE FROM THE TRAVELING MAN: THE TRAVELERS BOOK ONE

Twenty-five years later...

The Traveling Man, a con man currently going by the name Tom Brown, turned off the highway west of Seanboro onto the limestone gravel driveway marked by the bright red mailbox. At the end of the driveway sat a peeling, brown and white ranch-style house under a half-dead elm tree. He parked in front of the garage and got out of his black Cadillac Escalade, his leather briefcase tucked under his arm. For this job, he wore neatly barbered gray-black hair with a closely trimmed beard, fake horn-rimmed glasses, and a charcoal pinstripe suit. He stood by the car for a moment to collect himself. The morning sun was hot for September, and the air felt thick with pollen, but he took a deep breath anyway and exhaled slowly, falling into his role of land speculator, getting ready to play his part, before he walked across the gravel to the front door and rang the bell. An old man with red-gray hair thatched over a white, jowly face answered the door.

"Mr. Yost?" Tom asked.

The old fat man nodded his head. He had one hand on the door-jamb and the other hand on the doorknob.

"I'm Tom Brown. I spoke with you on the phone. Me and my associates are interested in the property you own on White Bear Lake."

The old man laughed. "I thought it was some kind of prank call."

Tom shook his head. "I assure you, Mr. Yost, that we are very serious."

Yost turned his head back into the room. "Mary," he yelled. "That fella is here about the property."

"Really?" she called back. "Well, the house is a mess. Go out to the picnic table."

Yost turned back to Tom. "Meet me at the garage."

The garage door went up. Inside, the garage was decorated like a porch. The room was paneled with vertical knotty pine boards. White curtains hung in the windows. In the middle of the room was a green wood picnic table that could have come from a city park. Two metal-framed folding chairs with a small white table between them sat to the left near the front opening. Yost hobbled down the steps from the house and indicted the picnic table with a wave of his arm. Tom sat down on one side. Yost eased himself down on the other side, gripping the table and grunting as he lowered himself. Mary Yost, stoop shouldered and white haired, shuffled out of the house. The screen door slammed behind her. She wore a button-up housedress with matching slippers and was carrying two glasses of ice tea. She set the glasses on the picnic table and sat down next to her husband. "Tea?"

Tom smiled. "Thank you, ma'am."

She nodded. "Garage is still cool."

Tom could feel the sweat at the back of his neck. "Yes, ma'am."

Yost took the other glass in both hands, took a sip, and set it down. "So what is this nonsense about the lake property?"

"As I said on the phone, I believe we can broker that property for you."

"Young fella, let me review the facts for you. My grandpa farmed that land, did well, but he and my pa didn't get along—"

"Too much alike," Mrs. Yost said.

"Too much alike. So when Grandpa retired, he leased it to the Air

Force. That was in about 1950. They used it for Cold War training—you know, secret hush-hush stuff. Congress put it on a decommission list about ten year back. After the Air Force left, we lost our income. Developers had big plans, especially for the lakefront. We put all our money in. Then some environmental folks said the land was contaminated, so we went after the Air Force for a cleanup."

Mrs. Yost cut in. "Air Force said the land was fine."

Yost nodded. "Judge ruled with them. So we should have had a happy ending, right?"

Tom nodded. "I know all this."

Yost continued. "But the county said, 'No, the paper says it's contaminated, dangerous to people, you cannot build.'"

Mrs. Yost continued. "We borrowed to fight the county, but it didn't do any good. Had to sell the big house to pay off the loans."

Yost looked Tom in the eyes, a big frown on his face. "So you're wasting your time."

Tom took a sip of tea. "Mr. and Mrs. Yost, me and my partners know your situation intimately. We studied everything in the public record. We believe we can overturn the county's previous ruling and get your property developed."

"We don't have any money."

"You don't need any money. Right now you've got nothing."

"Worse than nothing." Mrs. Yost chimed in. "We've got tax liability."

"Exactly," Tom continued. "We'll do whatever it takes: overturn the county, find a developer, get the legal paperwork done. In exchange, we take fifty percent on the sale of the land."

"Fifty percent?"

"We do all the work and pay all our expenses out of our half. All you have to do is sign this paper." Tom took a contract out of his briefcase. "It says that we have the sole right to act on your behalf in the sale of the lake property, that we pay all expenses—all of them—and that we receive fifty percent of the sale."

"Fifty percent is mighty high."

"We're taking all the risk. This is an expensive proposition."

Mrs. Yost glanced at her husband. "Right now we've got nothing."

Yost ground his teeth. "We should run this by our lawyer."

Tom shook his head. "This only works if it's all kept secret. Word gets out and enviro nuts start harping. I'll be honest with you: I can't guarantee you'll actually get what the land should be worth. I can just guarantee that you'll get as much as it's possible to get."

"As much as it's possible to get." The Yosts held hands.

"Give us a minute to read this contract." Yost took a pair of wire-rimmed glasses out of his shirt pocket, slipped them on, and started reading the contract, his finger moving along under the text while his lips moved. Mrs. Yost followed along over his shoulder, squinting while she read.

Tom sat back and sipped his tea. The sun was slanting into the garage and he could feel the sweat running down from his armpits. He got out his handkerchief to mop his brow. He hoped he hadn't sold them too hard.

The Yosts looked up almost at the same time and turned to each other. Mrs. Yost nodded her head slightly. Yost turned to Tom. "Okay, we'll sign. I'm just warning you that you're throwing your money away."

Tom handed him a pen. "We'll take that chance."

By lunchtime, Tom was sitting in a booth at the Superior Diner with his wife, currently going by the name of Patty, and their partner Buddy Ray. Patty was forty-two, but even carnies misguessed her to be five years younger. She was thin and willowy, with her dark hair cut short in a way that made her eyes and mouth seem more childlike. Today she was wearing a black skirt suit with a triple-strand gold necklace. Buddy, who sat across from them, was thirty years old. He was blond, heavily muscled, and wore a black crewneck shirt with a pair of khaki pants. Tom cut off a piece of his meatloaf, pushed some mashed potatoes on top of it, forked it into his mouth, and washed it down with a sip of iced tea. "So, the first step is taken care of. We are the sole representatives of Mary and Phillip Yost."

Patty picked at her salad. "And now we assemble the pieces of the puzzle."

Buddy set his half-eaten hamburger down on his plate and picked up a French fry. "I still can't believe we're going with the fifty-fifty split."

"There's plenty of money on this job. We'll take two hundred and fifty thousand, if it all goes to plan," Tom said.

"That's beside the point. We shouldn't leave any money on the table. We should always scrape up everything we can. You taught me that."

"Yeah. I also taught you not to get caught. The idea is to make this score look legit. It doesn't pass the smell test if we cheat the Yosts."

Buddy dabbed his French fry in the ketchup on the edge of his plate. Patty looked from Tom to Buddy. "It's time to move on, guys. We all know what you both think. It was Tom's call. End of discussion."

"Thank you," Tom said.

Patty continued. "So now we can take the soil cores, deal with the county environmental officer, find our local real estate agent, and work our magic on a developer."

"Yes, indeed," Tom said. He glanced at Buddy. "You got the coring equipment, the GPS locator, and the property maps?"

"Good to go."

"Then get started on the cores while we keep developing our cover. Lay a grid, get a sample from every square, document it all like a science project. This has to look convincing."

"Come on, Tom, that's a big-ass piece of property. It'll take days. It's all bullshit anyway. Can't we just make it up?"

Tom shook his head. "Want boxes of samples tied to locations. Want a thick wad of analysis. That's the amount of material that will enable the environmental officer to create a convincing story."

"If we get him on board."

Patty smiled. "*When* we get him on board. He's a divorced guy with two kids in college. He'll be jumping when I snap my fingers."

"So get the cores done," Tom said. "And then, for fun, you can find and corrupt our real estate agent. Sound fair?"

Buddy picked up his burger. "Anyone I want?"

"As long as she'll play ball."

Buddy bit into his burger. With his mouth full, he said, "I'll hold you to that."

Ten days later, Buddy was sitting in a dark back booth at the Home Run Bar and Grill, a sports bar in a strip mall on the west side of town that was a favorite hangout of real estate agents for Friday afternoon happy hour. He had a fresh haircut and shave, and his shoulders bulged out of his blue golf shirt and navy blue sports coat. The waitress who brought him his tap beer had eyed him over approvingly. He'd made a mental note to check up on her later. As he'd been sitting there, cross-checking the patrons against a computer listing of local real estate agents on his smartphone, the scene had become progressively more crowded and loud. After his second beer, with happy hour winding down, he noticed Marcie Tolliver standing by herself at the bar. She was as tall as a basketball player, busty, with auburn dyed hair and legs like an athlete. Her navy blue sports coat was a little loose and her khaki skirt was a little tight. He slipped up beside her, smiled when she glanced at him, and ordered another beer from the bartender. When he'd gotten his beer, he looked at her like he was seeing her for the first time. "How's it going?"

Marcie was sipping at a tall mixed drink. "Long day."

"Me, too." He looked her up and down. "Looks like we have the same taste in clothes."

She had a look on her face like she was going to blow him off, but after she saw his blazer and khaki pants, she said, "You're not wearing high heels."

He nodded. "The added height makes me too intimidating, so I have to stick to flats."

"I'm taller than you."

"Only in those heels, girlfriend."

She smiled. "You got your repartee going on." She shook the ice in her glass. "I haven't seen you around here before."

"I'm just in town with my partners working on a land deal."

"Really? You know this is the real estate agent hangout?"

"You're kidding. I thought agents were too competitive to hang out."

"You can't keep score if you don't hang out."

"Ouch. Now you're sounding a little bitter."

She drank off the bottom of her drink. "Like I said, long day. I've got to go."

Buddy stuck out his hand. "I'm Buddy, by the way."

She shook his hand. "I'm Marcie."

"Good to meet you, Marcie. Maybe I'll bump into you again."

She shrugged. "Maybe." She started to leave, but then turned back. "You really working on a land deal?"

"Marcie. So cynical. You must be having a bad week. Yeah, like I said, I'm here with my partners working on a land deal."

"What's that about?"

He shook his head. "We have to keep things quiet, or you local wheeler-dealers will cut us out. See, you're not the only person who knows what a bad week is."

She took out a business card and handed it him. "Well, if you need any local info, call me and I'll give you the skinny."

"Thank you, Marcie. I appreciate that. You have a good evening."

He watched her walk away. She was already hooked; she just didn't know it. Her career wasn't going very well and she was sitting by herself in a bar where she should have friends or be making friends. Probably wasn't cut out to be a real estate agent. But she did have an agent's license. And in the very near future, she was going to have some new friends and opportunities she'd never dreamed of.

***

Thanks for reading this sample. *The Traveling Man: The Travelers Book One* is available at major book retailers.

FINALLY...

Thanks for reading *The Double Cross*. If you enjoyed it, please post a review on the review site of your choice. A few words will do. Honest reviews are the number one way I attract new readers. Thanks so much.

I'd love to hear from you. You can reach me at my website: https://michaelpking.org

The Travelers
The Double Cross: A Travelers Prequel
The Traveling Man: Book One
The Computer Heist: Book Two
The Blackmail Photos: Book Three
The Freeport Robbery: Book Four
The Kidnap Victim: Book Five
The Murder Run: Book Six
The Casino Switcheroo: Book Seven
Thicker Than Thieves: Book Eight
The Dark Web Scam: Book Nine

www.ingramcontent.com/pod-product-compliance
Lightning Source LLC
Chambersburg PA
CBHW021116130626
46554CB00002B/715